Love and HIPLIFE

First Published in Great Britain in 2020 by
LOVE AFRICA PRESS
103 Reaver House, 12 East Street, Epsom KT17 1HX
www.loveafricapress.com

Text copyright © Nana Prah, 2020

ISBN: 978-1-9163628-1-9
Also available as ebook

ACKNOWLEDGEMENTS

My gratitude overflows to Love Africa Press for believing in the story and publishing it.

I've said it once and I'll say it a million times more, my editor Zee Monodee is the absolute best!

I'd like to thank Empi Baryeh and Amaka Azie for your honesty as beta readers.

Thanks to Estelle Kramo who helped with the Cote d' Ivoirian French lines in the story and for introducing me to her beautiful country when I went to visit.

The Arabic lines were initially vetted by my good friend Mario Iseed, who has wanted to be a character in one of my books ever since he learned I was a writer. Maybe one day.

DEDICATION
To the late Professor Joseph Kwesi Ogah. He will always be one of my favorite educators.

CHAPTER ONE

Climbing Mount Afadjato, the highest mountain in West Africa, wasn't the grandest objective Lamisi Imoro had ever come up with but at this point, she'd die before she got to the top. If only she could suck in enough air, she'd be able to at least take another step.

"Oh, God. Oh, God. I … can't …"

She planted both hands on her knees so she wouldn't crumble to the ground in a heap of blubbering sobs. How many people had the young guide seen keel over in their pursuit of the climb? Why the hell did he have so much energy to leap up the incline when taking four steps knocked the wind out of her?

Her best friend, Precious Kpodo, turned and retracted the few prized paces she'd gained towards the top to return to Lamisi's side.

"I told you we should've waited until your cold cleared," Precious said as she her chest rose and fell with her own heavy breaths. "To be honest, with all of that yellow mucus you said you were bringing up last week, I think you have a touch of bronchitis."

Now able to stand without pain slashing through her ribs with every inhale, all Lamisi could do was glare at her friend. "You're a physiotherapist, not a doctor."

Precious was right, but Lamisi hated being sick and would go to any length to make sure it didn't disturb her life. Ignoring it helped it to go away faster.

She kicked at a stone on the ground. "I swear this mountain has plotted to kill me so it can reign victorious over my downfall."

Precious laughed. "You'll be all right. Take one step at a time and think about dancing on the highest point in Ghana."

Her body, now caught up with its much-needed oxygen supply, gained vigour with the desire to accomplish her task. She thrust her shoulders back. "I can do this. I can do anything I set my mind to."

She clambered up the near-vertical gradient that should've been outlawed for people to climb. Each forward motion turned into a burden that brought fire to her lungs as she breathed in what should've been cool forest air.

Always searching for unique and fun things to do in Ghana, she'd arranged the weekend trip to the Volta Region.

No more mountain climbing. Ever.

She tugged her sweat-drenched T-shirt away from her chest as she stopped again, panting with the effort to catch her breath. "We're almost at the top, right?"

The guide's empathy must've disappeared after her nonstop complaining because he didn't look the tiniest bit sorry when he pointed straight up and replied, "We've gone a quarter of the way. It gets steeper from here."

Earlier, he'd mentioned winning a competition last year amongst all the guides by climbing and descending the mountain the fastest.

Lamisi released a whimper of anticipated torment.

"I can't go on. You two can leave me here. I'll be fine." She waved a hand towards the scenery. "I'll enjoy nature."

And inhaling without effort.

Precious and the boy shared a look. "You know we can't do that. They told us at the information desk that we had to stay together. If you want us to go back down, we'll do that. This was your goal, not mine."

Damn. Precious knew just how to get to her. Holding in her grumbles of complaint, she trudged forward.

What had to be an hour later, she paused and glanced at her watch. Only a miserable five minutes had passed.

Heavy footfalls caught her attention as another group trooped up behind them. She recognized the trio of men led by their own guide—they'd left them at the hotel. How had they climbed so fast?

She'd never been one to go fan-crazy, but her first sight of Bizzy, ingeniously pronounced *Busy*, one of the most fascinating hiplife artists to catch her ear, had left her speechless. The musical genre blended Ghanaian culture with hip hop beats.

Being in the same room with him had had her hands trembling while her heart beat out of sync. Her face had most certainly turned all shades of reddish brown with the effort it had taken not to bounce up and down while screaming.

Not even seeing him in concert several times through the course of his career had caused such a reaction. Watching his videos captivated her like no other musician ever had. Not that she spent much time gawping at his tall, muscular body as he did things with his hips that had saliva easing out the side her mouth. Once. It had happened just once.

He'd winked at her when their gazes had caught and held in the hotel lobby. Hadn't it been enough that her belly had done some kind of crazy flip and she'd gotten dizzy? She'd transformed into a flirtatious, bold woman as her eye had repeated the motion. Never in her thirty years had she winked at a man.

During the brief interaction, she'd wanted to run to him and gush about his music and then ask for a picture with him, of him, near him.

It hadn't happened. She'd taken the coward's way and swiped the smile off her face and endeavoured to put on an aloof air with her head high and shoulders thrust back. So what if that move had made her breasts lead her out the door and his eyes had fallen to them?

It wasn't the Ghanaian way to throw oneself all over stars.

First of all, it created way bigger egos than they needed. Second, she wasn't a groupie trying to get into his bed. Although thinking about what those hips could do made her want to reconsider the stupidity of not introducing herself to him. Who didn't like having fans?

Not that she'd know. Her life revolved around teaching languages and doing research for her PhD. No fandom there.

The tall, broad-shouldered man possessing brown eyes with the clarity of a Malta Guinness glass bottle caught her attention while still a few feet below her. His decadently full lips rose at the corners, revealing white teeth that contrasted with the richness of his russet-brown skin. Judging by how his eyes narrowed as his cheeks pushed them up, his smile must be genuine.

She couldn't breathe for a different reason other than climbing the wretched mountain.

Lamisi pivoted to face her nemesis and trudged upward. To relieve her mind from her inability to take in full breaths, she counted each step. Maybe by the time she got to a hundred, they would've reached the top. Wishful thinking.

She'd made it to twenty before grabbing onto the backpack she'd thrust at Precious when things had started to get rough. If the woman could drag her to the top, everything would be fine, but Precious swatted her hand away.

"I'm not a cart donkey, Lamisi. I'm barely able to get through this ordeal myself."

Lamisi had trouble believing the words. Precious' skin glistened while Lamisi had gone through three face towels—one of them Precious'—and removed the bandana she'd used as a headband to cover her twisted natural hair in order to dry her face.

Precious continued up the pathway, and just as Lamisi was about to do the same, the second party walked up behind her. Having lost the competitive edge to make it to the top before them ten steps ago, she did nothing but shift to the side as they proceeded.

They didn't pass. Bizzy himself stopped next to her.

"Good morning," he greeted in an ultra-sexy voice.

Maybe the exertion of scaling this beast of a mountain wasn't so bad if it could make his voice a bit huskier and breathier than his singing voice. Not a huge difference, but her ears caught and wanted more.

"Are you all right?"

Lamisi tore her gaze away in an attempt to not stare like some silly school girl with a crush on the most captivating man she'd ever encountered. "I'm fine. Just taking a breather."

Before he could respond, one of his companions spoke in Hausa, a language of some people from northern Ghana. Individuals from ethnic groups in the middle and southern areas of the country didn't tend to speak it. He obviously presumed neither she nor Precious understood.

Lamisi looked down at her chest and crossed her arms over her breasts. *Crap.* Exercise plus cool mountain air equalled nipples which could double as headlights through her T-shirt. Why hadn't she thought to wear a padded bra?

Bizzy chastised the guys in Hausa about their rude behaviour and warned them to cut it out.

The giggling men continued to gossip about her, but she was happy he'd tried to stop them.

She sucked in a lungful of the cool air before speaking her next words in Hausa.

"I would appreciate it if you would stop talking about my breasts as if it isn't a natural phenomenon for them to react to the cold." She felt a moment of pride over having pulled out the equivalent of a word in a language that wasn't her first, or even her sixth. "As your friend pointed out, it's rude to talk about people in a language you *presume* they don't understand." She thrust a finger into the air. "It's impolite to talk about people in any language."

She hoped bird poop would land in their gaping mouths as she turned her back to them and climbed with the renewed intention of reaching the top.

The run-in had ignited her temper and reminded her that she was a strong woman. She might not be able to control every aspect of her body or her life, but her mind was another matter. Where her thoughts went, her body would follow. Right then and there, she mentally catapulted herself to the peak. Nothing would stop her now.

***

Blaise Zemar Ayoma, known to the world—or at least the hiplife-listening crowd of Ghana—as Bizzy, snapped his mouth closed and stared at the retreating back of the curvaceous woman. Her facial features and accent when she'd spoken to him in English had delineated her as someone who wasn't from his ethnic group or at least hadn't grown up among them. Yet, she'd understood and spoken Hausa fluently.

He whipped around to his friends and spoke in English. "How many times have I warned you about discussing people in front of them in Hausa? Now you've upset her."

Their raucous guffaws bounced off the trees.

Abdul, his oldest friend and trusted bodyguard when the need arose, cupped his hands a few inches from his chest. "But her nipples within her perfect breasts were pointed straight at you. Didn't you notice?"

He certainly had. His semi-aroused state would attest to it, but he'd never admit it. Her smile and wink that morning at the hotel had charmed him. He'd decided to introduce himself when her demeanour had changed. A scowl had contorted her face before she'd huffed out of the place.

Both women were striking, but in very different ways. The speaker of his native tongue was shorter, the crown of her head reaching the top of his shoulder. Standing at six feet, he'd been born the runt of the family. Even his mother towered over him.

The woman's compact body and flawless skin presented as someone who took care of herself. Anyone who understood that natural hair was beautiful was the kind of woman for him. Not that he'd decline someone who used relaxers or wore weaves, wigs, or extensions in their braids, but he had an affinity for the confidence it took for a female to wear her hair in its original state.

Her bright dark eyes had spoken to him, called him. Unfortunately, his friends had messed it up before anything could get started.

"You need to apologize," he ordered.

Musah ignored him. "Maybe you excited her, and that's why she was showing them off."

He tried again. "I know you heard me. We'll march up there, and you'll apologize."

Abdul nodded his agreement while Musah mumbled something about women being nothing but temptation.

"Don't you even think about making her your third wife, Musah."

The man tilted his head and looked to the sky as if contemplating it, and then shook his head. "Kadijah and Hawa would kill me. Besides, the woman isn't my type. Much too severe and talkative for my liking."

More like bold and brave for addressing something that bothered her. Qualities that appealed to Blaise.

"It makes no difference." Abdul pointed to his skull. "Her tight, short-sleeved shirt, jeans, and lack of hair covering indicates she doesn't share our religion. I don't believe such a woman would be persuaded to become a Muslim."

"You know that not all women wear hijab, so she could be Muslim." Blaise grinned. "If you two apologize, then perhaps I have a chance with her. At least to go out on a date."

Both men scoffed. Musah clapped a hand against Blaise's shoulder.

"You don't have a chance, my brother. Don't forget that you are also a Muslim, although a backsliding one. Besides, that woman would deliver you to an early death with her words alone. My ears are still ringing from the inflection she used in our dialect. And you know she's not from our area. Imagine what would happen to you if she chastised you in her own language?"

Abdul shook his head. "My friend, it would deteriorate your manhood. You need a calm woman to suit your laid-back personality. One who will support your career and not put her own above yours. A good Muslim woman like your parents expect you to marry."

Blaise's heart sank. How many times had he heard the same edict about marrying within his religion, his culture if possible, from his mother?

He longed to push aside his friend's words, but he knew them to be true. He didn't need a dramatic woman who would trouble him. Not with the media trying to dig up information on his lifestyle that wasn't any of their business.

Although he hadn't practiced the faith consistently in years, he shivered at the thought of his parents' reaction to him bringing home a woman who wasn't Muslim. Their support over the years had been immeasurable. He never wanted to disappoint them. He had a certain image to uphold as the child of a chief. His father had been generous in allowing him to fulfil his passion of becoming a hiplife artist. He wouldn't push the boundaries. His wife would be a Muslim, with no argument.

The woman with peaked nipples and the contagious smile had interested him. Not just with her fluency in Hausa, but her initial friendly response to him at the hotel before shutting down. But his friends were right.

"You still have to apologize," he reminded them.

Musah dropped his hand to his side. "Rightly so. That's if she doesn't collapse by the time we reach her."

The two men laughed while concern made him want to get to her faster.

CHAPTER TWO

Lamisi allowed her outrage to carry her battered muscles and tortured lungs to the top of Mt. Afadjato with only one more break. She refused to let the uncouth men catch up with them.

When they finally reached their destination, she stumbled to the rock formation where the signpost announced the altitude of eight-hundred-eighty-five metres and allowed her legs to buckle.

Precious snapped a few pictures of Lamisi's final demise before handing the camera to the tour guide and posing for her own pictures.

The stunning view left her mesmerized. Had it been worth a near-death episode to experience one of Ghana's natural wonders? She'd have to ponder it once oxygen had replenished her brain.

Precious took the camera from the guide and settled next to her. "Now that you can breathe, tell me what happened with those guys."

When Precious had asked her on the way up, Lamisi had chosen to focus on placing one foot in front of the other. She now told the story of their rudeness.

Precious laughed. "I didn't even notice."

Lamisi blew out a gust of air. "It's not funny. It was embarrassing."

"At least you have nice breasts."

They glanced down at her chest. She'd placed a couple of tissues over her nipples to keep them hidden.

"I do."

"The guys were cute," Precious said.

"For bush men."

Lamisi bristled when she noticed them clear the corner to reach the top. Hand slapping ensued among them.

She gathered the strength to stand. "Time to go."

Precious turned her attention to the copse of trees leading to the end of the climb. "Don't let them spoil your victory of making it up here. Relish it. How about taking pictures where you don't look as if you've passed out?"

"You're right. I must look victorious for social media." She stood next to the signpost, placed her fists on her hips, and focused straight ahead at the clear blue sky. "Snap away."

The trio headed in their direction, looking as if they'd taken a stroll on flat land rather than the gruesome incline Lamisi had endured. She tried to ignore them, but had a tough time keeping her gaze away from Bizzy's commanding presence.

After more than enough pose changes and a few pictures taken by the guide with them together, she hooked her arm through her best friend's and walked to the edge overlooking the town. "I wonder if the people down there think anyone is watching them."

Precious chuckled. "We can see houses and cars, but the humans are dots from this distance. I'm trying to figure out how many of them have ever climbed this mountain."

"I'd guess very few."

The sudden presence of a voice smooth as whipped shea butter made them both jump.

Bizzy held up his palms. His crooked grin did more to increase Lamisi's heartbeat than his sudden presence in their conversation.

"I'm sorry. I didn't mean to scare you."

Not feeling charitable towards him or his crew, her tone came out harsh. "It's not polite to eavesdrop."

He dipped his head forward in acknowledgement. "It seems that our transgressions against you are piling up."

"This is your first offense." She waved a finger at the two men standing on either side of him. "Unlike them."

The one with the lightest skin amongst them all stepped forward. "We're sorry to have offended you. If we knew you understood our language, we would never have done it."

Lamisi fought the upward twitch of her lips at the withering look Bizzy shot his friends. She craned her neck to look into his eyes. The men held the characteristic height of those from the most northern regions of Ghana.

"Is it right to talk about people in a language they don't understand?" she probed. "I was taught that it was bad-mannered."

Before either of his two friends could speak and dig themselves further into their trench, Bizzy shook his head.

"What he meant was that he shouldn't have been speaking about you at all, especially about something so—" His eyes twinkled as his tongue flicked out to lick his tantalizing lips "—sensitive."

Lamisi feared she'd collapse with the sudden thinness of the air. She refrained from looking down at her breasts to make sure her hardened nipples weren't poking through again. With one word, he'd aroused her. Well, one word said in the sexiest voice she'd ever heard.

Unnerved, she'd gain control by informing him that he shouldn't be the one apologizing, but Precious pinched the back of her arm.

"She accepts your apology."

"Thank you." He spoke to Precious before turning his attention to Lamisi. "My mother always tells me that only people with big hearts are able to forgive. My name is Blaise Ayoma. These are my friends Abdul Fobil and Musah Adongo."

Lamisi allowed Precious to be their spokesperson since she wasn't as ready to forgive as her friend had indicated. She'd rather put the men on the hot seat and enjoy watching them squirm for a little while longer. At least until they realized their offense.

Precious touched the tips of her fingers to her upper chest. "I'm Precious Kpodo, and this is Lamisi Imoro."

Blaise looked into Lamisi's eyes when held out his hand. "It's a pleasure to meet you."

She wiped her moist palms on her sweat-soaked jeans before sliding the right one against his. An unexpected electrical current coursed its way up her arm and down her spine. She swallowed hard, enjoying the odd combination of pleasure and awareness inviting her to move closer.

"It's ..." She cleared her throat when it came out raspy. "It's nice to meet you, too."

After longer than what seemed normal, they released each other, and he offered his hand to Precious. Lamisi extended hers to the other two men in turn. She noted that the contact with them didn't do anything but make her want to wipe their dampness from her palm. There was no desire to bask in the attention of their gazes like she'd wanted to do with Blaise.

Standing within arm's length to one of the greatest hiplife artists in Ghana, her tongue loosened. "I'm a fan of your music."

And you.

No need to reveal the silly crush she had on him. As a musician, not a person. She didn't know him like that.

A lopsided grin appeared. "That's good to hear."

Not what she'd expected. His modesty elevated her attraction to him. As an artist, not a man whose handsomeness stole her breath.

Precious pointed and squeaked. "Oh my goodness. You're Bizzy."

Her friend had never been good with faces, but it had taken her long enough to recognize him.

All three men beamed, making her wonder how the sun reflecting off their teeth at such a height didn't temporarily blind her.

"My friends call me Blaise, so feel free."

Lamisi bit the inside of her cheek to keep from laughing at Precious' besotted gaze.

She fought her own giddiness as she thought about his accomplishments. He'd struggled for years before making the charts two years ago with his hit song, *I dey gaya da nokwrɛ*. The translation of *I tell you the truth* didn't sound as rhythmic as when he sang in the four languages he'd used.

English, Pidgin English, his own mother tongue of Hausa, and Twi, the most spoken local language in the middle and southern portions of Ghana.

The song impressed her more each time she listened to it. Not only did the beat have her wiggling her hips, but the lyrics were insightful in a way that few people could understand unless they spoke all four languages. Which she did, with an addition of seven others.

His songs tended to possess a powerful depth that most people had limited understanding of because of the mix of languages.

On the surface, his music appeared light and fun as he sang about a love which has been lost or found, enjoying life, or some other frivolous theme. Those who could interpret the words understood that he incorporated politics, issues of social justice, and even the overuse of religion in the system as undercurrents to his lyrics.

She hadn't wanted to know if he wrote all of the songs himself. Already holding him in high regard, she didn't need her awe and fascination of him rising to the stars.

She turned to Precious and tugged at the hem of her shirt to stop from lifting her friend's chin to close her mouth. "Are you ready to go?"

It took a few more seconds of staring before Precious turned her attention to her. "Pardon me?"

"Let's head back down."

Never shy, Precious held her phone to Lamisi before asking Blaise, "Can I please take a picture with you?"

"No problem."

Precious pointed to the signpost. "Over there."

Once they reached the spot, Blaise draped an arm around her shoulders.

Lamisi placed a hand over her stomach at the surprise burn of jealousy in her stomach. She stood rooted in place and snapped several pictures instead of charging to the pair to pull them apart.

"That should do it," she announced.

Relieved when they separated, she reached out to hand Precious the device.

Blaise stayed in place and nodded at Lamisi. "Would you like a picture, too?"

Saying no would be rude, wouldn't it? She handed Precious her phone. With each step, she hoped he would loop his arm around her, too. But then, she recalled her sweat-soaked shirt and recanted the wish.

He didn't seem to mind her sopping-wet clothing because he tucked her into his side. She snaked her arm around his waist and gripped his shirt as she leaned into him. Despite a height difference of at least half a foot, her curves fit into his firm body as if they'd been pieced together in a puzzle. Heat burned the side in direct contact with him, and she snuggled in closer as he squeezed her shoulder.

A part of her hoped the photo session would never end. The muskiness of his perspiring skin blended with the spiciness of the cologne that clung to his shirt had her inhaling deeper. If he smelled this amazing after having climbed a mountain, he'd be irresistible when freshly showered and dressed.

Women threw themselves at the star for a reason. Hell, she'd become one of his groupies for a moment. Who was she trying to kid? She still was. Yet, no matter how friendly, handsome, or talented he was, they came from two different worlds within the same country. He lived for people to watch and admire him while she preferred to stay in the background, observing. She'd do best to remember how different they were because their relationship would never last.

As if there was a miniscule chance of him thinking about me in that way.

When Precious announced that she was done, Lamisi released her arm from around him and started to move away, only to be held in place.

He handed his phone to Musah. "Take some with mine."

Lamisi craned her neck to look up at him. "I'm not famous, like you. What do you need my picture for?"

The intensity in his eyes softened her knees.

"It's only fair," he stated in Hausa.

He had a point.

"And you feel too good against me to release just yet," he added.

He couldn't be serious. The line would work on one of his younger groupies. Her maturity kept it from going to her head. "I'm sure you say that to all the women you pose with."

His brows drew together as he canted his head in thought. "No. Never. You're the only one."

A warmth that had nothing to do with the sun radiated out from her chest. The ego of a simple woman who spent all her time with her head buried in journal articles researching for her PhD and teaching language courses wanted to believe him. Her rational mind kept her connected to the reality of him being a charming man who knew how to weave words into entrancing spells.

"Share your beautiful smile with the camera. And me."

His whispered words breezed into her ear eliciting a delicious shiver.

She looked at him to see if he'd taken his own advice. Her lips complied with his instructions when she discovered him focused on her. Smiling.

"I've snapped at least twenty pictures. I'm done," Musah said with a scowl directed at Blaise that hadn't been present before he'd been given the job of photographer.

Lamisi shuffled away from the electricity of Blaise's touch. She regretted the loss of contact.

"Thank you for the pictures," she said in a rush to leave the man who set off an unfamiliar desire in her to plaster herself against him. Possibly press her lips against a mouth which sang lyrics that had the power to touch her heart with their conviction.

She pointed towards the centre of the earth with her left hand and waved with the right as she back-pedalled to where they'd come to flat ground.

"We're heading back down, so enjoy the rest of your stay."

Blaise caught up to her. "Would you ladies like to join us for lunch when we reach the bottom?"

He'd used the breathier, huskier timber from when they'd first spoken on the way up. If exertion hadn't caused it like she'd thought, what had? Was he flirting with her?

Goosebumps erupted at the possibility. She had to get away before she begged him to say her name. Maybe whisper it and then have his tongue trace along the shell of her ear. She shivered and crossed her arms over her chest to hide any evidence of her reaction.

Her enamoured state came to a screeching halt. Hadn't she read or heard somewhere that he was getting married to a Nigerian heiress?

She answered his invitation before Precious could. "Thanks, but we have to get home. It's a long journey."

"Where do you live?"

She looked at Blaise from the side of her eye. "Why do you ask?"

His muscular shoulder rose in a shrug. "If you're going to Accra, you could ride with us. Unless you drove."

His friends stepped to either side of him.

"There's no room," the tallest said. "Not with our wives."

She had her reasons for getting away from Blaise; what was theirs? "We drove, so there's no need for the ride."

"Thank you, though," Precious said with a huge grin. "It was generous of you to offer."

Blaise's gaze never left Lamisi's face as he held up his phone. "Can I have your number?"

She blinked several times. *What the hell for?* She'd never been and never would be a home wrecker. She didn't believe in disrespecting herself or her fellow sisters.

She snarled in disgust. "I'm sure your girlfriend wouldn't appreciate that."

She grabbed Precious' arm and called for their guide who stood watching the scene.

Lamisi led the way, not waiting for anyone's response to her comment. She would've loved the chance to interrogate him about his insightful lyrics, but knowing he'd be willing to cheat on his girlfriend, a beautiful heiress who ruled social media, set a blaze of ire in her belly.

What a philandering jerk.

CHAPTER THREE

Lamisi found the descent a hundred and fifty percent less tiring than the climb, yet more treacherous. She slid a few times as the stones and dirt shifted under her feet, before wizening up and slowing her pace rather than rampage down the mountain to get away from a certain womanizing hiplife artist.

A patch of dirt loosened as she stepped down, causing her foot to resist gravity and kick into the air with the other soon to follow. A strong grip stabilized her and kept her from hitting the ground. Heart beating with a bounding so intense that it hurt her ears, she looked up to thank her rescuer. The words got stuck in her throat as she met the handsome face of the man she'd stormed away from.

Forgiveness for the way he'd disrespected his girlfriend with his blatant flirtation had yet to enter her consciousness. She pulled her arm out of his grip and mumbled, "Thank you."

Then, she turned ... only to slip again. *Dammit.* This time, she regained her balance without help.

"Take your time. There's no rush."

Ignoring how his presence, to her annoyance, made her stomach flutter, she took more careful steps.

He hitched a thumb behind them. "We were getting along well. What happened up there?"

A direct man. Of course he was, because how often did talented, outrageously gorgeous, communicative men drop into her life?

"Why did you ask for my number when you have a girlfriend?"

"I'm a single man."

He was a performer—the sound of surprise and conviction in his voice could be an act. Yet, he hadn't hesitated for even a second before answering. It wouldn't be the first time she'd come to the wrong conclusion about a person, but her source had been reliable. Kind of.

"That's not what the entertainment news report." She placed a hand on her hip as he stepped closer to her so that Musah could get past. "Deola, the Nigerian oil heiress? Remember her?"

Abdul laughed as he slapped Blaise on the back. "I told you that escorting Deola to those functions would come back to haunt you."

And then, he continued on his way, leaving them planted on the side of the mountain.

Lamisi watched the others meander towards their destination as she waited for Blaise's answer. Precious was in the midst of pointing at a tree as she chatted with the tour guide. The woman loved all things science.

He shook his head. "I'm not dating Deola. Or anyone else right now."

"So she's not your girlfriend like the tabloids say?"

Why should she even care? They'd just met, and unless she attended another one of his concerts, they wouldn't see each other again.

"It was a misunderstanding."

By this point, she had heard enough. She turned to make her way down the mountain so she could get as far away as possible.

"We aren't dating, but we sort of use each other."

She nodded as she tried to convince herself that she didn't want to hear the whole story. "Thank you for clearing that up. I wish you two a happy life together."

He skittered past her and blocked her path. "Please, let me explain."

She crossed her arms over her chest and tapped her foot out of annoyance, but disappointment held a bigger portion of her current emotional state. She'd rather have never discovered that her hiplife hero was a plain human male who made bad decisions without caring who he hurt.

"What for? I'm someone you just met. It's not necessary. Besides, I'm hungry."

His full lips spread into a smile as he took off his backpack. Curiosity got the best of her as she watched him open it and pull out a chocolate bar.

Blaise waved it in front of her face. "I'll give it to you if you listen to my explanation."

Her stomach grumbled loud enough to scare the hidden wildlife as she eyed the candy with longing. What would it hurt to hear him out? She'd get some gossip directly from the source and a snack to tide her over. No negative in that equation.

He reached for her hand and placed the chocolate in it. The tingles skittering up her arm from the contact overtook the sensation of hunger.

He hesitated for a moment before shaking his head with a deep frown. "I'm sorry. I don't know what got into me. I should've just offered it to you without the bribe. It was nice meeting you, Lamisi."

Then, he swept his hand to indicate that she should walk ahead of him.

She hesitated for a moment before opening the candy bar. "You're invited."

He chuckled and shook his head to decline. "Thank you."

The tradition of offering to share food tended to be a source of entertainment. What was the saying about sharing being caring?

She took a bite and moaned as the flavour of the peanuts, caramel, nougat, and chocolate merged onto her tongue as the most decadent treat she'd ever eaten. Hunger made everything taste incredible.

"Thanks," she said around the confection still in her mouth.

His Adam's apple bobbed several times. "My pleasure."

Never had words felt as if they'd stroked her most intimate places as delicious warmth settled low in her abdomen. She glanced at her chest to ensure that those well-placed tissues were still doing their job. Barely.

The quicker she got away from him, the better.

"Look, your life is none of my business." She pointed in the direction they were supposed to be headed. "How about if we complete the descent so we can go home?"

He didn't speak as he stared into her eyes, seeming to consider her for a moment.

After long seconds of his direct attention, her mouth went dry as she longed to close the gap between them and feel his body against her again. Tilt her head up and stand on her toes so she could kiss him. Just once because her tingling lips needed to know.

A photo of Deola, resplendent and regal in a splendid silver gown while she hooked her hand into the crook of Blaise's arm at a gala, burst into her mind.

She averted her gaze and set her feet to walking.

"How do you understand Hausa?" he asked after a few minutes of their feet crunching against the earth.

Heat infused her face despite there being no exertion as they strolled. The question never failed to embarrass her when it should be a source of pride. People tended to question her honesty when she discussed her language skills so much so that she never wanted to. Explaining that she was a genius when it came to linguistics was too much of a hassle.

"It's one of the languages I speak. I picked it up when I spent a few months in Nigeria. Bauchi State in the north." A short and simple answer that should lead to no more questions.

His jaw dropped, exposing all of his teeth. "You learned Hausa in a few months?"

She nodded, ignoring his astonished tone. "I've always been good with languages."

"How many do you speak?"

She sighed in resignation at having to carry on with the conversation. "I speak eight languages fluently. I'm not counting pidgin."

She kept the fact that she understood a total of twelve to herself. That part tended to freak people out.

She snuck a glance at him as she waited for his reaction. Would he call her a liar? Or try to test her with any of the other languages he might speak?

The corners of his lips were downcast as he nodded and kicked at a stone on the path with his shoulders hunched forward. "More than the five I know."

It sounded like he might be jealous. The man had talents that transcended hers in so many ways, and he was envious of her ability with languages. She transitioned her snicker of delight into a cough.

She expected at least one question from him about her language skills. But nothing broke the silence apart from the crunch of the ground caused by their steps.

Her curiosity made her ask, "What's your fifth language?"

He rubbed his chin. The combination of the trimmed beard with the faded haircut suited him.

"French."

Her love of his music and languages got the better of her. "Ah. *As-tu déjà pensé à l'intégrer à ta musique?*"

A slight horizontal crease appeared on his forehead when his brows rose. "I understood the word music."

She spoke in English. "I asked if you had ever thought of adding French into your music. You don't speak any French at all?"

He shrugged. "I started taking lessons with a private tutor a couple of weeks ago. I'm moving into the next phase of my career by having French be the base of some of the songs I'm writing. It'll make me more accessible to the Francophone countries."

Did she dare ask? "So, you write your own lyrics?"

His shoulders appeared broader as his chest expanded. "I do."

She pursed her lips to the side, not quite believing him. "You wrote the songs on all three of your albums?"

"You really are a fan. People remember two. That first one went nowhere."

"I know, but in my opinion, it was the best. The nuances you put into the lyrics were insightful. More than just a beat. Even though those were catchy." She ignored the slight slip of her sneaker. "You didn't answer the question. Did you write all of the songs yourself?"

"Every single one. No artist is an island. My producers had input when it came to laying the tracks."

She looked into his eyes. Did she believe him? Why shouldn't she? Not as if she found him to be unintelligent, but to be so graceful with words, not just in one language, but three or four in the same song, was beyond belief. It must be similar to the astonishment people experienced when they learned about the number of languages she spoke.

A few paces passed before a melodious tune swirled into her ear and captured her attention.

"When I looked into your eyes for the very first time, I was swept away by their intensity. They were so open one moment and then shuttered closed the next. I wanted to get to know you, but you were gone. Until we met again on the mountain climb."

Her body became weightless she got a sense of floating. Bizzy had just serenaded her with a song she'd never heard before. He'd created it on the spot about their encounter. Three languages interwoven into one beautiful set.

"How did ..." Incredulous at his amazing ability to weave words on the go in a way that sent chills down her spine, her extensive vocabulary vanished.

He shrugged. "Creating songs is my gift."

Gazing into his eyes with admiration, she didn't see the tree root jutting out in the middle of the path until it was too late.

Considering he was staring at her instead of where they were going, for once, he was the one to trip over the obstruction.

She reached out to grab him liked he'd done so many times for her. But the contact she made with his muscled arm wasn't enough.

Relativity kicked in as time moved in super slow-motion.

Rather than reversing his downward momentum as she'd hoped, she descended with him.

With a turn of his head, he must've realized she was chasing him down on the ride. Then, he did the most incredible thing.

In one fluid movement, Blaise grabbed her with both arms and pulled her close. His solid bulk took the brunt of the interminable fall when they landed.

Still, gravity wasn't through with them as they rolled a few times together ... until they finally stopped.

CHAPTER FOUR

Blaise opened his eyes with a start once they stopped tumbling. On any other day, a beautiful woman lying on top of him would be welcomed. Concern for her wellbeing hit him harder than he had the ground.

"Lamisi." He loosened his arms from the tight hold and lifted his head to look at her. "Lamisi," he said a little louder.

Her groan caused a sense relief that had him taking full breaths again.

"Are you okay?" he asked.

He winced as she adjusted herself against his chest and raised her upper body to look into his eyes.

"As far as I can tell. What about you?"

His buttocks throbbed, but he wouldn't share that. "I'm sure that even with my brown skin, I'll be bruised tomorrow from the fall."

She reached a hand to the ground to help push herself off of him. He held her in place with a light hold. The warmth of her soft lushness had the effect of some sort of anaesthesia against any pain he hadn't assessed yet.

"If you release me, I'll get up. I know I'm not light."

He stared into her eyes. "You're just right."

Her heart thumping hard against his chest increased its pace, and her breathing became shallow and rapid as her gaze dropped to his mouth.

Electric shocks swarmed along every inch of his skin. If nothing else ever happened in his life, he had to taste her. Relish the fullness of her lips. Lose himself in the reality that made up the woman he'd just come to know as Lamisi.

He raised his head to meet her flesh. The spark at their contact shot into him. But he only had the chance to experience a lingering soft brush of her tantalizing lips as she pressed against him for too short a time.

Then, she scrambled to her feet and shuffled backwards.

He sprung up to make sure she didn't fall again. Bad move. The pain had him seeing full daylight under the canopy of trees as his ankle gave way. He landed back on the ground.

Lamisi rushed to him and knelt. "Are you all right?"

He sucked in a breath. "My ankle. I think I may have twisted it. How are you?"

Other than kissably gorgeous.

"You broke my fall, so I'm fine." She touched his shoulder. "Thank you."

As a man, he couldn't let her get hurt for attempting to help him when she didn't have to. "Anytime."

When the warmth of her hand seeped into him, he realized just how much he meant it.

Once again, she was the one to break the intoxicating moment between them. "Let me look at your ankle."

She shifted down to his foot, pulled the hem of his jeans up, and then grazed her fingers along the area just above the rim of his sneaker.

A red-hot tearing pain bounded around the spot. He tried to stifle the hiss, but it escaped as he pulled his leg away from her.

"It's already swollen. It could be a severe sprain or a break. I'm not sure. I'll run down and get Precious so she can check it out." Her hand landed on his knee as if to reassure him. "She's a physiotherapist."

Terror clawed at him as he thought of her going down alone. Possibly getting injured. "It might be nothing. I might've just been surprised the first time I stood. Let me see if I can put pressure on it."

Her eyes went wide and her twists shook with the swing of her head side to side. "I don't think you should. You saw how well I did trying to stop your fall. Neither of us needs to take another tumble like that again."

Unless it's into my bed. He shook the intruding thought away while the creative side of him made a mental note to write a song using the word tumble.

"I'll be okay." There was no harm in trying.

Blaise ignored Lamisi's extended arms as he pushed himself up onto his strong leg. He did accept her shoulder to rest against as he lowered his injured one onto the ground.

He closed his eyes against the excruciating shards of pain and lifted his foot before he could place his full weight on it.

"Oh, dear Allah in the Heavens," he said in Hausa.

"I would've thought you'd be using some swear words," Lamisi said.

Grateful for the support, he glanced down at her. "I don't curse."

"Is it a side effect of following Muslim rules?"

He grinned. "If you want to call my mother's chastisement and punishment of uttering it a side effect, then so be it."

She laughed as she helped him sit on the ground.

He grunted as he gingerly settled his leg in front of him.

"Keeping my language clean was one of several stipulations she gave me when I told her I wanted to go into the music industry." He caught her gaze. "That, and making sure to respect all women."

"Sounds like she's strong and instilled some good values into you."

Proud of his mother's achievements when it came to educating the women in her town and those surrounding them in the Northern Region of Ghana, he smiled. "She is."

Lamisi pulled out her cell phone. "There's no signal. I'm going to get Precious and the tour guide."

Having no other choice but to let her go, he grasped her hand and squeezed. "Be careful."

"I will. I'll be right back."

He watched as she descended. Out of sight, he tested the ankle by moving it. He let out the growl of pain he hadn't been able to express in Lamisi's presence.

And then, he relaxed or tried to while he waited for help to arrive.

Sure, he'd just experienced agony like he couldn't recall in years, but he'd also just had the ultimate of sweet kisses. Something that wouldn't have happened if he'd been paying attention to where he'd been going rather than staring into her enthralling dark eyes.

His lips still tingled from the brief touch. He wanted more. To make it a deeper encounter and have her respond to him rather than run away.

As much as she might want to deny it, she liked him. At least, she'd been impressed with his music. Always a plus.

Already, she'd inspired him to write. Tumble was the word she'd thrown at him. Which language would he use to describe his plunge into her eyes and seeing straight to her soul?

He'd always been told, especially by his stern disciplinarian of a father, that he was emotional. He'd learned over the years how to take advantage of it through poetry, and eventually, his lyrics, rather than be ashamed. He understood his feelings, and with Lamisi, he'd definitely toppled into something he'd never experienced before.

CHAPTER FIVE

Lamisi rubbed her arms as the sensation of needles pricked into her skin. She had to look down to make sure they weren't real. She hated hospitals. No, not even close to the word. *Detested, deplored, despised* all rolled into one would better suit her feelings about the institution. She still hadn't gotten over childhood incidences of treatments and injections which had supposedly been meant for her own good.

"Are you okay?" Precious asked as they sat in the waiting area of the Emergency Room while Blaise's two friends had gone to his bedside.

She lied with a nod while clasping her trembling hands together. She wouldn't be okay until the disgusting antiseptic scent left her nostrils.

Precious shook her head with a deep frown altering her beauty. "I'm surprised you volunteered to join us."

"What was I supposed to do?"

She kept her voice low, out of earshot of Abdul's and Musah's wives. The youngest one kept glaring in her direction. Not the first time a Ghanaian woman had given her nasty looks she didn't deserve. It wasn't as if she'd pushed Blaise and laughed over him in victory. Lamisi ignored her.

"The guy broke my fall by letting me land on top of him." For a moment, her nausea receded as she recalled his heroic action along with a kiss she'd never forget.

For those few seconds in his embrace, she'd allowed herself the luxury of believing that only they existed in the world. The craving she'd experienced to get even closer had magnified by a thousand as she lay sprawled on top of him. That kiss had been inevitable.

Or so she allowed herself to believe because her stomach roiled with the wretchedness of her guilt. She'd kissed another woman's man. If he couldn't say outright that he wasn't dating Deola, then it meant they were. Having been cheated on by two guys in the past who she'd thought she'd been seriously involved with, she never wanted to make another woman experience the same type of detrimental betrayal at her hand.

"Let's go." Her friend's voice jogged her mind into the present. "I came to make sure he got the X-ray. We don't need to wait." She raised a finger and moved them left to right in Lamisi's face. "Your phobia of hospitals is making your eyes look glazed."

Lamisi blinked several times.

"I don't have a phobia." She rubbed damp palms against her jeans. "Just a debilitating fear."

Those last words had come out as a mumble.

Precious considered her.

"And yet, instead of staying at the hotel, or even in the car, you decided to come in. Interesting," she drawled out.

"You had to be there to see the acrobatic feat he performed." Lamisi rolled her hands around themselves, failing to replicate with their motion what had happened. "Escorting him here was necessary."

Precious nudged her shoulder with her own. "You've had a crush for years. He's gorgeous, successful, and from what I observed, seems to like you, too. A guy doesn't stare at someone like he did you unless he appreciates what he sees."

Wait until she told Precious about the kiss, the impromptu song, and Deola.

Her shoulders slumped at the last. "Let's stay a little longer. I want to find out how his ankle is. I hope it isn't broken."

What could she do for him if it was? Nothing. Why was she fighting nausea and a possible fainting spell by hanging around?

"I doubt it, but it's better to be sure. You look more green than brown right now. Let's go see how he is so I can get you out of here."

Every muscle in her body had become sore as if she'd been, well, climbing a mountain. She wasn't sure if her jittery legs would be able to support her if she stood. She shivered as sweat meandered down the side of her face from the terror threatening to drown her.

"I hate hospitals."

Precious looped a comforting arm around her shoulders. "I know. That's why you being here for him is so shocking. You like him, don't you?"

"I respect his music. It's incredible. Most people don't recognize that he's taken a social stance while dancing to his songs. Not until he gives his interpretation during an interview. Plus, he protected me when he didn't have to."

Precious raised a brow. "Weren't you the one trying to stop him from falling when he tripped?"

She wasn't having that conversation again. Nor would she admit that she liked him. It didn't matter, anyway. He was making his way up the music charts while she'd be completing her doctorate within the year. They lived completely different lives, and other than being multilingual, probably had nothing in common.

Then why was she still sitting in this dreaded hospital waiting for him?

"Help me up. That mountain did bad things to my legs, and I'm not sure I can walk anymore after sitting for so long."

Precious laughed. "What makes you think I can get up myself?"

Lamisi's breath snagged as her attention caught the hiplife star hobbling down the corridor. "Here comes Blaise with his friends."

At the sight of him without plaster of Paris on his lower leg and supported by Musah alone, she forgot the soreness of her body, stood, and went to him.

"So, it isn't broken?"

His charming crooked smile eradicated the misery she'd suffered through while waiting.

"No. Badly sprained, though."

Relieved and unable to keep her hands to herself when she'd been so worried, she reached out and touched his arm. She wasn't sure who passed the current, but she took a moment to enjoy it before letting her arm drop. "That's great to hear. Much better than a break."

His eyes captured hers and refused to release her. "You stayed?"

"Yes." She ignored the heat creeping up her neck and hitched a thumb at Precious. "She wanted to make sure they treated you well."

Precious cleared her throat.

So what if she'd just revealed her true feelings to her best friend with that tiny lie? She'd deal with the teasing later.

He shifted his eyes away, leaving her with a longing to bask in them.

"Thank you, Precious."

"No problem. It was actually—"

"We need to go." After years of friendship, she knew when Precious was about to rat her out. "It's a long journey to Accra. And you should get off your feet. I hope you'll be able to elevate your leg while you drive back."

"He'll be fine," Musah said. "Let's go."

Blaise raised his leg. "Lamisi has a point. The doctor instructed me to keep it up and iced."

Not wanting to leave him, she lunged at the opportunity. Nothing prevented her from getting to know him. As her favourite musician.

"Since it's just Precious and myself in her car and yours is full. How about if we give you a ride?"

A choking sound came from Precious.

Blaise cut off anything Musah had opened his mouth to say. "I accept. It'll give us a chance to finish our discussion."

CHAPTER SIX

Blaise lounged in the back seat of the Kia Sportage SUV. That new car smell permeated his nostrils as the air conditioning cooled the atmosphere. He had his long leg extended along the backseat without it touching the door as an ice pack sat on top of his ankle.

The medication they'd given him had taken the edge off the pain. He no longer winced each time he adjusted his leg. From his vantage point behind the driver's seat, he observed Lamisi's profile while she kept her sights on the road. Her forehead sloped into a pert nose that shadowed a slightly smaller and darker top lip than the pinkish-brown bottom.

His lips tingled as he recalled the pillowy softness of hers during their fleeting kiss. He wanted more. Not just physical encounters, but to get to know the beautiful woman. He had no doubt her personality would be gorgeous, too.

"Tell us *all* about Deola," Precious said after she'd gotten them fifteen minutes into their journey.

He glanced over his shoulder to find Abdul still on their tail in his Land Rover Discovery. He anticipated a heated lecture for the stunt he'd pulled. It would be worth it if he could get Lamisi to go out with him on a date. His instincts screamed in a way he couldn't ignore that getting to know her would change his life.

They could hang out and indulge in the heat of attraction that ignited when they got close. Perhaps if they fell in love, she'd be willing to convert so they could marry. The possibility pleased him.

As if ice water had been thrown in his face, he realized that he'd never visualized marrying anyone before. He'd just met Lamisi and knew little about her. The medications must be stronger than he thought to allow him to have such ridiculous musings.

"Are you okay?"

He snapped out of his thoughts to find Lamisi's concerned gaze focused on him.

"Yeah." He grimaced as he rubbed his thigh, hoping they'd think it had been pain that had let his mind stray. What had Precious asked? Oh, yes. About Deola. There isn't much to tell about Deola. She's all over social media and what you see is what you get. High fashion and travelling."

He'd leave out the negative aspects that she didn't show everyone. Her persistence in having her way all the time rivalled that of a manipulative politician. She was spoiled, rich, and controlling. Not a good combination for anyone who had to deal with her.

Precious clicked her tongue. "I meant about you and her. It's rumoured that you're together."

He was sure Deola had started it, but he had no proof. It was ironic that they'd come out after she'd started dropping hints that she liked him in more than a platonic way.

"We're friends. The media made more out of our attending a few events together than they should've. As you know, she's the heiress to an oil empire. With me being the son of a prominent chief, they called me a prince. The concept of a royal romance in modern West Africa appealed to them, and obviously, their audience."

He caught the way the women tipped their heads towards each other and exchanged a glance. He didn't question it. The media had promoted the rumours with enough verve to make it seem believable.

Lamisi angled her body with her shoulder propped against the back of the seat. Her eyes narrowed as if she had the power to see through him like the X-ray machine they'd used on his ankle. "The tabloids say that you're dating exclusively and are on the cusp of getting engaged."

He maintained eye contact to help provide support to his words. "That's not true. We're only friends. Nothing more."

"Benefits?" Precious asked.

He shrugged. "That's none of your business."

The women exchanged another poignant look.

"But no," he admitted. If he wanted to see Lamisi again, he had to be transparent. "We're two people who hang out every once in a while when there's a special occasion with press hovering."

No need to tell them about the time Deola had kissed him. The memory still left a sour taste in his mouth. Her beauty and elegance hadn't stirred anything in him. Attraction had to be present—in their case, it proved missing.

"At glitzy events," Lamisi muttered as she settled into her seat, facing the windshield.

"It helps to hang out with someone who knows the business. Her father may be an oil mogul, but she's into hanging out with celebrities. Her social media numbers are through the roof. It never hurts to be seen with her."

Precious' brow rose as she glanced at him in the rear-view mirror. "Are you using her?"

"Not at all." He had difficulty finding a way to explain. "We've just never addressed the rumours with the public. Denying anything to the media triggers them to latch onto it. We both know it'll die down."

Unless Deola feeds into it.

Lamisi returned to looking over the side of her seat. Probing him. When she seemed appeased with the truth in his answer, her lips curved up into a smile. A good sign.

"How did you meet?"

"At a party Wander threw in Nigeria about a year ago. He introduced us, and we got along."

The car swerved towards the left before Precious corrected it. "*The* Wander?"

Blaise chuckled. "The one and only."

He'd had similar reactions when he'd met his favourite artists for the first time. The humbling experiences had given him the insight into why people stumbled over their words when they came in contact with him.

Lamisi's eye roll before she resumed her proper seating position showed just how impressed she was with his name-dropping.

"Who is the song 'A friend forever' about?" She carried on with the interrogation.

His lips puckered into a frown, and he blinked several times at the mention of a single from his first album that never got radio play. The fact that she was able to rattle off the title so readily let him know how much she appreciated his music. Warmth swirled beneath his ribcage and settled in the centre of his chest.

"It was released years ago, so it couldn't be about Deola." He skirted the question.

She nodded. "True. Precious, please pull over."

Her friend did a double take in her direction. "Why?"

"I'm getting a crick in my neck from turning so much. I'm going to sit in the back with Blaise." She looked at him. "If that's okay with you?"

The anticipation of having her closer elicited tingles all over his scalp similar to what happened every time he went on stage.

"Sure," he said in as casual a manner as he could manage.

Precious slowed down and pulled over to the side of the road. Women carrying one-man-thousand and abolo on their heads ran to the vehicle. The miniscule fried fish paired with the steamed corn and rice flour wrapped in banana leaves were popular in the area.

Lamisi climbed out of the vehicle, opened the back door, and assessed the situation.

With a twinge of pain, he moved his leg to the floor to give her space, and she got in. Once settled, she patted the top of her thighs. "I'll be your pillow."

For someone who knew how to create and spit out lyrics with the ease of breathing, he sat speechless.

"It's okay," she coaxed. "I know one of your legs probably weighs as much as both of mine, but I'll be fine. If it gets to be too much, I'll return to the front."

"The added elevation is good for your ankle," Precious contributed as she removed her wallet from her bag.

He placed his limb on her. Electric shocks infused into him from the heel of his bandaged foot to where their contact stopped mid-calf.

For the first time, he thanked Allah for the injury he'd sustained. This might end up being the best car ride of his life.

CHAPTER SEVEN

The intimacy of them in the backseat ensconced in a way that people who had known each other for years would engage in should've been uncomfortable.

Not even a little bit. The weight of Bizzy's leg settled on her thighs set off a familiarity that she wanted even more of, so she took the liberty of resting her hands on top of his lower leg.

The tantalizing sparks of awareness where they touched made her breathing shallow and rapid. She'd hyperventilate if she didn't gain control of her body, so Lamisi ducked in deep inhales and releasing them slowly.

What had she been thinking by getting so close to him? Her heart hadn't settled into a normal rhythm since they'd sat in the same car. Now, she doubted that any part of her body was getting enough blood with the speed the organ was racing.

That's right—she had wanted to ask her favourite artist questions regarding his work that she was sure no one had ever queried him about before.

Precious caught her attention in the rear-view and smirked as if she understood the lies in the excuse her mind had created.

Now that she knew he didn't have a girlfriend, she'd ceased fighting the magnetism pulling her closer to him as if they were each tied to an elastic cord that had reached its peak stretch. A wonder she hadn't crawled on top of him already.

Precious waved towards the sellers surrounding them. "Do either of you want abolo and one-man-thousand?"

Lamisi snapped out of her daze of sensation. "I almost forgot that Alhassan asked me to get him some. He can eat two big bags of the one-man-thousand in one sitting. Please get me enough of the fish and of the abolo to keep him happy."

She didn't miss the tightening of Blaise's calf muscle against her. When she gave him her attention, he was staring at her with a tight frown.

Without thinking, she rubbed her fingers along his shin. "Are you in pain? Should I go back to the front seat?"

His muscles clenched again at her touch, and then relaxed.

"No pain," he said in the husky voice from their mountain encounter.

His fingers as they grazed her arm spiked a barrage of incredible sensations that caused goose bumps to burst out onto her skin.

"Stay," he whispered.

The dry state of her mouth made it difficult to speak, so she nodded.

Oblivious to the fireworks going off in the backseat of her car, Precious asked, "Blaise, do you want anything?"

His gaze remained steady on Lamisi. The passion that filled his eyes as the tip of his tongue licked his lips enticed her. Of its own accord, her body leaned closer to him. One more taste wouldn't hurt. Their first kiss, although nice, hadn't satisfied.

Halfway toward her destination, Precious' throat-clearing jarred her out of the craziness she'd been about to indulge in, and she sat straight up.

"Fish or abolo is what I meant by *anything*."

"Nothing for me. Thank you." His low tenor voice brought to mind hot nights entwined with a lover who could satisfy.

Lamisi tore her gaze from those succulent lips to view the cement buildings outside her window as she fanned her face. The same woman who was quick to remove her hand from a person's grasp during a handshake had been about to initiate a kiss. It had to be the combination of physical exhaustion and the remnants of oxygen deprivation that had her acting so out of character.

Or she'd finally come into contact with a man she had a hard time resisting. Considering that his upper body had risen towards her as she'd closed in, it had been a mutual moment of yearning.

Precious looked between them with a grin before ensuring that the food she'd placed in the passenger's seat was secure. And then, they were back on the road heading to Accra.

"Who's Alhassan?"

The hardness in his voice caught her attention more than the inquiry. Was he jealous? It would explain the initial scowl and the tension in his muscles when she had mentioned the name.

She'd asked him quite a few personal questions already. Only fair she reciprocated. "My older brother."

His head jerked back as if surprised. "Alhassan is an Arabic name."

"It can be." Just because she'd give him the information didn't mean she'd make it easy to learn more.

"Are you Muslim?"

As always, the question asked by someone she barely knew irritated her. What did it matter what name she called God or how she chose to worship as long as she treated people with respect, love, and dignity?

"My mother was a Muslim before she got married."

She'd asked her mom several times why she hadn't maintained her religion. Her answer had always been about love and sacrifice. She'd discovered a better life by converting in order to be with her husband rather than to live without him and remain a Muslim.

"She insisted on naming her children, though."

He leaned closer with interest. "Your name is popular in the north of Ghana."

"She's Dagomba from the Northern Region."

"Do you speak Dagbani as part of your language repertoire?"

Precious interrupted with her laughter. "Don't even bother asking her that again. Any language you can think of, she probably speaks, understands, or can pick up in like two minutes."

Lamisi denied with a shake of her head. "That's not true."

"Close enough."

Blaise's grin took the sting out of her embarrassment.

"If I had your skill for languages, I'd—"

"Become an international spy? A quadruple agent?"

He chuckled. "I was thinking more along the lines of writing songs in lots more languages. But being a spy might be fun. Are you one?"

Making sure her face remained neutral, she cocked her head the slightest bit as she stared at him.

"Do you think I could tell you if I was?" And then, she giggled. "I can't lie to save my life. With me, what you see is what you get."

"I'm pretty sure there's a lot to learn." He winked. "I'm looking forward to taking up the task."

Either he was a great liar or he really did like her. Would he ask her out when they dropped him off, or was he all talk? The real question raced within her bounding pulse. Did she want to see him again?

To her credit, Precious kept her mouth closed.

"Back to your siblings. How many are you, and what are your names?"

It was as if he knew she didn't know how to handle the flirtation.

"We're five in total. The eldest is Alhassan, then Miriam." She pointed to her chest. "I'm right in the middle. Then comes Ras, and the baby is Amadu."

"What do you all do for a living?"

She raised her right hand from where it rested on his leg. Her palm cooled when a second ago, it had been absorbing his heat.

"Your turn. Remember that's why I came back here in the first place?"

Precious' snicker was the only indication that she'd been paying attention to them. Where was a divider when you needed it? Lamisi wanted Blaise to herself.

Realizing the possessiveness of her thoughts, she rested her hands at her sides, limiting their contact. She needed to keep a clear perspective, and touching him any more than necessary blurred her reasoning.

He raised a brow while the corner of his lips twisted towards the side in confusion. "What was the question?"

She laughed at his adorable expression. "Since your memory is so poor, I'll refresh it. Who did you write 'A friend forever' about?"

And are you still in love with her? Pining for a woman who doesn't return your affections?

She wouldn't hold it against him if he didn't answer. It wasn't any of her business. She chewed the inside of her cheek as she willed for him to appease her curiosity. The song beheld a haunting melody, and the lyrics had touched her at a time when she'd fallen in love with a man who never saw her as more than his student.

Time had healed her from the, but regret still lingered at what could've been whenever she saw him.

Had Blaise gotten over his own heartbreak, or was his heart still beating for another?

"What if I just made up the song?" he asked.

"I could be wrong, but I don't think that's your process. Your music sounds personal." *And touches my spirit with their depth.* "Nothing can convince me otherwise, especially after hearing the song you created before we fell."

His dark eyes seemed to consider her. Or had his mind wandered to the past?

"It's about someone I loved and lost."

Precious snorted. "Is that how you're going to play it? Lamisi picks up nuances in languages like the skin absorbs sun rays on a bright day. She likes your music because of the meaning you attach to it. Unlike most people, we don't understand every language you sing in. She does."

Lamisi nodded at her friend's support.

"Besides," Precious continued. "If you haven't guessed, you've just met your number one fan."

Those appealing lips rose into a smug smirk, adding a gleam to his eyes. "Is that so?"

Her face heated to feverish levels as she ducked her head.

"She is. She's been following you ever since she heard the first song you released. I'm surprised you don't recognize us from your concerts. She's dragged me to at least five of them."

Not needing any more mortifying truths to spill from her friend's mouth, she gathered her courage and looked Blaise in the eyes. "It was for research purposes."

Not a complete lie, if years ago she'd been to a psychic who had foreseen coming up with an idea for her doctorate based on his music.

"Uh huh." The disbelieving murmur from the front seat wasn't helping her case.

"Your songs inspired me to write my PhD dissertation on the use of mixed languages in music and the impact on the listener."

His smile broadened.

"I don't know what impresses me more: myself for inspiring you, or the fact that you're studying for your PhD."

"Since I have your injured ankle in my lap, if I were you, I'd praise me going for my doctorate."

He touched his hand to his chest. "But my magnificence brought it out in you. I deserve the credit."

Lamisi giggled. "You're right. It's all about you. Years of coursework, intensive research, writing, and disappointing mishaps that waylaid my progress with a year left, if I'm lucky, before I stand against a panel to defend my work means very little."

"When you put it like that ... How about we share the accolades?"

She tipped her head from side to side as if considering. "Sounds fair."

"Have you really been to five of my concerts?"

"Yes," Precious answered. "We flew out to Lagos for one of them. She knows all of the lyrics and could sing your songs if you ever got sick."

"Precious," she hissed. "Please don't let me inform Blaise about some of the adventures I've had with you over the years."

Her oldest friend caught her gaze in the mirror and clamped her lips together. The smile of mischief stayed in place.

"So, Lamisi Imoro is my number one fan." He reached out to her. "It's nice to finally meet you."

She glanced down at his palm and then back at his earnest eyes before shaking it.

Without warning, he tugged her to him and whispered, "Gorgeous and intelligent, with a great ear for music. A magnificent combination. It would be my pleasure to get to know such a spectacular woman better."

Her heart took off at a gallop as electric currents shot up her arm and charged her whole body. A slight turn of her head would place her lips against the bristles of his short, well-kept beard.

She struggled to haul in a breath. What was the response to someone she'd crushed on from afar for years?

"Um ..."

His mouth against the shell of her ear sent feathery flames along the area with every movement of his lips.

"It's okay. We can take our time and see what happens. I wanted you to know that I like you."

His withdrawal left her filled with longing. For once, a man's direct approach hadn't irritated her. In the short time she'd known him, he'd done nothing but impress.

CHAPTER EIGHT

Lamisi had asked him to share one of his deepest secrets. That took confidence. For both of them.

"You asked me about 'A friend forever'."

She nodded.

He wiped a hand down his face. Was he really going to do this?

"Most people presume it's a song about friendship, but there are two lines within the lyrics that reveal the truth."

"*One day, the time will come when ...*" she recited in English then continued in Ewe as he'd originally sung it. "*My broken heart will mend.*" Then, "*From your inability to love me as more than a friend,*" was completed in a perfect Nzema accent.

Did she realize that she'd placed her hands back on his leg? Her gentle touch exposed how lost she was in the words.

She looked into his eyes. "They were the only lines I have ever heard you sing in Ewe and Nzema. As if you'd learned the languages just for the song."

He grinned, proud of her ability to comprehend more than the lyrics, but the depth of them. "I wanted to sing about my unrequited love, but not have people truly understand."

"Give me the full translation in English," Precious ordered.

Instead of speaking the words, he sang the song in English the way he'd written it, but then hidden it with Ewe, which he spoke fluently. The words sung in Nzema, spoken by an ethnic group in the Western Region, were all he understood of the language.

"Awww. That's so sad," Precious said with a hand at the centre of her chest. She took a second to turn to Lamisi. "I can see why it hit you so hard back then."

Blaise shifted his gaze between the two. "One-sided romantic experience?"

Lamisi cleared her throat. "I'll share if you will."

Did he really want to hear about her past loves? Could he afford not to? What if she were still hung up on this guy?

"Mine was nothing major," he said. "One of my college classmates saw me as nothing more than a friend."

"You wrote a song about it and veiled the lyrics in languages you don't use. Doesn't sound minor to me."

He shrugged. "What's in the past is done."

"What happened to her?" Precious asked.

"I don't know. We didn't maintain contact."

Because I couldn't watch her go out with other guys knowing one of them would be the lucky one to win her heart.

Lamisi looked at him. "Are you still hung up on her?"

He chuckled.

"Not at all. It happened years ago. What's that saying about time healing all wounds? It surely does." He pointed at her. "Unless it didn't for you. Are you still in love with the guy?"

Her twists shook along with her head. "Not at all. Time truly is a cure-all. At least for relationship issues."

One question pressed on him that he needed an answer to. "Are you involved with anyone right now?"

She snapped her eyes to his. He expected an indignant refusal to answer.

"No."

His chest collapsed as the air he'd been holding in rushed out. "I can't tell you how glad I am to hear that."

***

Blaise's talent as a musician had always been obvious to Lamisi, but she wouldn't have guessed he'd be quick-witted and hilarious. The banter between the three of them had her ribs hurting with laughter. The return trip had taken much less time than when they'd driven up.

Wasn't it always the way that the journey home seemed shorter than when heading out to an unknown destination?

Precious parked in front of a house set in an estate complex in Tema that Blaise had directed her to. Aside from the differences in colour, the homes, from what she noticed above the protective wall, appeared similar. The area was pretty, with trees planted along the sidewalks and clean, but bland. At least on the outside. The interiors of the properties were probably as unique as the owners.

What would Blaise's home look like? She'd guess cool and comfortable. Like how it felt to hang out with him. Then the practical part of her brain smacked down her romantic one, and the word *flashy* came to mind. He had the means, so why not show it off, right?

Lamisi looked down at the weight on her lap. Her own legs had gone a little numb, but she'd refused to give up the proximity.

"How's the ankle?"

"For right now, I'll say its fine. I have a feeling that as soon as it touches the ground, the pain will be excruciating."

She stroked the top of his foot and said a silent prayer for healing. "You'll be better sooner rather than later."

"Thanks."

A knock sounded at his window. His friends and their wives were lingering outside.

He pressed the button to slide the glass down. "Give me a minute."

Not waiting for a response, he rolled it back up, pulled out his phone, and placed his thumb on the finger scanner to open the screen.

"How about we exchange numbers?"

Filled with uncertainty, her hand flew to her hair and smoothed down the twists on the right side of her head. "I don't think that's a good idea."

Precious opened her door. "I'll be back. I'm going to stretch my legs."

She got out and closed the door, leaving them alone.

Traitor.

He rotated the device end to end several times. "I thought we were getting along."

Rejecting him might be easier if he wasn't still resting on her.

Who was she kidding? The necessary task of declining his interest would be difficult regardless. She lived a life of complete privacy. From what she knew about the stars in Ghana and the world, they existed in the spotlight, seeking attention everywhere they went. She had no desire for that.

"We were."

He raised his phone and wiggled it. "Then can we chat?"

Only one way to shut it down. "Look. You're a fantastic musician, and I love your work. Meeting you has been wonderful. Thanks for answering my questions about your songs, but we live in two completely different worlds."

He turned his head side to side and looked around. "Aren't we still on Earth?"

An exasperated sigh hid her entertained smile.

"You know what I mean. Your lifestyle is all flash while mine is as simple as khaki trousers." She flung her vision to the front to avoid the heaviness of his gaze. "I'd like to keep it that way."

"My life isn't as crazy as you're making it out to be. For the most part, I'm a normal guy when I go out in public. Ghanaians don't make a big deal about seeing me unless I'm on stage. They have more important things to concern themselves with, like their own lives."

He had a point. And he would know his lifestyle way better than she would.

"I already told you that I like you, Lamisi. It would be great to get to know you better."

His words had hit her straight in the chest. She liked him, too. Beyond his musician status. He was a down-to-earth man who was easy to talk to.

Yet, the fear in her gut churned. She couldn't risk the pain that getting to know such a man would eventually entail. As stereotypical as it sounded, she didn't doubt that he had more than his share of women and was able to toss one out when bored because so many others had lined up to fill the role. She had no desire to compete. Would she even be able to?

"You should let your friends help you inside and put some ice on the ankle."

His shoulders slumped. "So I can't convince you to give me your number?"

Already regretting her decision, she gave him a negative shake of her head.

"How about if I give you mine? There's no harm in that, is there? If you want to ask me more questions about my music, I'm at your fingertips."

A risk-free venture. "Aren't you afraid that I'll sell it to the highest bidder?"

"Just make sure you give me my share of the profits if you do."

Back to being comfortable with him, she grinned. Maybe she'd given him enough negative responses for the day. What would it hurt to have his number? She grabbed her cell from the space next to her. With her mind a little hazy from excitement, it took two attempts to slide the pattern onto her screen to unlock it.

Where was that *contacts* icon again? She located it and tapped. "I'm ready."

She input the number as he rattled it off. *Blaise.* What more did she need to add as she saved it?

"It was a pleasure meeting you, Lamisi. I hope you call and we get to see each other again one day. If we don't and you're ever at my concert, please come backstage."

Her mouth went dry with the temptation of the offer.

"By the way," he said and then paused.

"Yes."

"Let it be known that your lap doubled as the absolute best pillow. If you happen to hear it in a song, you'll know where it came from."

She laughed. "Just as long as you give me my share of the proceeds."

The joviality they'd experienced on the ride lingered until he tipped his head towards the glass.

"My friends aren't the most patient people, and I'm sure they're exhausted."

"You must be, too."

He lowered his leg to the floor of the vehicle. Try as he might, he wasn't able to hide his gasp, and she felt for him.

"My body might be a bit sore, but thanks to a beautiful, strong woman who kept me distracted from the pain, I've never felt more energized."

Wouldn't he stop his stream of lovely words so she could leave him without feeling the need to use the number he'd given her?

"Take care, Bizzy."

Just like when he'd first met her, he winked. "You, too Lamisi Imoro, master of many languages. I really hope I hear from you."

Unlikely, but she did, too. Sometimes, she longed for things that weren't good for her. He'd been flung to the top of that category.

They opened their doors. When she stepped out, she held tight to the metal as her legs buckled for a second. A quick glance over her shoulder revealed that no one had noticed because they were too busy helping Blaise.

She walked to his side to get some blood circulating to her weakened muscles. Getting one last glimpse of him.

Hobbling with support, he waved. "I'll be waiting for your call."

She raised her hand in a goodbye gesture before they escorted him up the walkway to his front door.

Misery over leaving a man she'd known for less than a day trumped the joy she'd felt while being with him. There was one thing she knew for certain. The man had captivated her.

CHAPTER NINE

A week had passed since Lamisi's trek up the mountain had ended in a roll down its slope with a stunning man to break her fall.

Blaise still stayed on her mind. It might be easier to forget him if she'd stop listening to his music on repeat. Each song fascinated her with the strength of his lyrics and the artistry involved in their creation.

Much to Precious' annoyance, his number sat unused on her phone. Lamisi had stared at it enough to memorize it. Yet, she never pressed the button that would have his smooth, low tenor voice sending tingles traipsing across her skin as he spoke.

She shouldn't be focused on a man when she had a doctorate to complete. Since she'd registered for the programme, the process had been thrown off the tracks not once, but twice.

Her principal supervisor had been brilliant—a linguistic studies professor who was knowledgeable, kind, and direct. Lamisi had always known where she stood with Professor Ogah who never wasted her time. Efficient and dedicated to academia and helping others to progress to their highest level. After a year of coursework, she had been assigned to him.

Towards the third year of her PhD and blissfully working on her dissertation, he had died after undergoing a minor surgery. She'd mourned him with the intensity of losing a beloved father figure. A tragedy not just for her, but the world because he had been such a spectacular individual.

Her second supervisor of the three she had been assigned had had to step up. A stressful time that she never wanted to repeat. It would've been better if her new supervisor hadn't even taken on her project because a year later, the woman had transferred to a university in Spain.

Where was the justice? Lamisi had been shot down so low that she'd spent a full week in bed crying, whining to anyone who would listen, and contemplating her educational goals. A master's degree wasn't something to sneeze at. It wouldn't get her to the level of academia that she desired, but she could live with it.

No, she couldn't.

She had set a goal of obtaining her doctorate, and nothing would stop her. As long as she had breath in her lungs, she would complete her dissertation, no matter how much time it took.

By the time her third supervisor had made himself available, she'd had to extend her program, which meant paying an extra year of tuition. Her doctorate would take five years instead of four. Not fair, but what could she do?

Professor Amartey was the kind of person who didn't want anyone rising up the ranks to meet his own. He hadn't thought her original topic was good enough and had wanted her to adapt her theses into something that would suit him.

Lamisi had been driving home, dejected after a meeting with Professor Amartey, when a Bizzy song had come on the radio. She'd wondered how many people understood the three languages he'd sung in.

The brilliant topic idea would appease Professor Amartey without her having to completely change her dissertation. She'd never forget the joyous desire to hop out of the car while dancing to the music as the vehicle moved forward, just like in those video challenges.

When she'd presented the idea to him last month, his frown hadn't seemed as negative as usual when he'd nodded his approval.

To this day, her hands still trembled when she walked into his office. The man hadn't become less intimidating in the least.

Between hospitals and having to see Professor Amartey, she wondered which one she hated more. At least, hospitals made it their mission to help a person feel better. Not so much for her supervisor.

Taking a deep breath to help calm her racing heart, she knocked on his office door.

At his gruff "Come in," she forced her feet to move.

"Good afternoon, Professor Amartey."

"Sit down," he grunted without looking up from whatever he was reading.

Not put off by his lack of greeting, she walked to the closest chair, swept her dark blue, knee-length skirt under her legs, and lowered herself down, placing her ever-present research notebook on her lap, and waited. Sometimes, it took up to five minutes for him to address her again.

In an ideal world, she would've requested a new supervisor who showed more respect for her and her work. Heck, in a model world, Professor Ogah wouldn't have died, and people would be calling her Dr. Imoro by then. She just had to endure for a short while longer.

He slammed the draft he had insisted she print out each time she submitted her work on the desk. "Your dissertation lacks depth."

She gripped her notebook instead of grabbing the stack of papers and kept quiet. He would explain in his own time.

"You mentioned an artist in the background of your work as influencing the topic of your research." Professor Amartey rested his forearms against the surface of his desk. "Along with the interviews of music listeners, you need to add interviews from performers as an aspect of your research."

Standing and screaming at the top of her lungs while taking her work and beating his desk with it wouldn't begin to satisfy her rage. Her nostrils flexed in ways she had no control over as she huffed in breaths to control her temper. She glanced down at her notebook to find it twisted.

Interviews with artists meant having to undertake analysis that took up so much time and energy that it would leave her fatigued for a full week once she completed it. Her mind blanked out for a moment to stop from thinking about the amount of work the man had added to the pile already on her head, ready to compress and then break her spine.

She flexed her fingers, hoping it would be enough to keep her from diving towards the man and placing her them around his neck. The university looked down on counts of assault and battery. It would better than letting the burning in her eyes give way to tears of frustration. Professor Amartey fed on weakness, so she sat with a stiff spine and kept her eyes dry.

"It's a great idea," she said without enthusiasm or honesty. As she'd experienced previously, there would be no point in arguing with him. "I also think it will add another dimension to the research."

Which was true. Even though it would suck up her time and brain power when she was already running on fumes.

"Bring the questions to me this week so I can review them, and you can get the interviews done as soon as possible."

Had he given a viable time-saving suggestion instead of grunting a goodbye? If she had heard the word e-mail in the sentence, she would've run out of the room screaming about an alien abduction.

"Yes, Professor."

Now to find some way to get in contact with the artists. It wasn't as if she ran in their circles.

Her breath hiccupped as Blaise's face grinning up at her just before their lips brushed hers sprang into her mind. Her heart pounded out his name in rapid succession.

Lamisi's brain whirled with the new development. Working tirelessly on a dissertation for so many years had made her a bit jaded. Just like that, her interest in her research had been rejuvenated.

Or is it the chance to talk to Blaise again?

She ignored the inner voice.

Would he connect her with other artists and allow her to interview him after the way she'd blown him off? She sure hoped so because she had no contacts in the music business.

Self-preservation had been a good-enough reason for her to stay away from Blaise. Completing her dissertation represented a greater incentive to call him.

It didn't mean anything would happen between them, though. For the sake of her doctorate and avoiding bias, nothing could.

***

Blaise sat with his French tutor, bored out of his skull. He'd been deceiving himself when he'd presumed that the language would be easy to learn and incorporate into his music.

The six weeks of these three-hour lessons four days a week had been a waste of time as his mind swirled with the differences in tenses. Why would they torture people by assigning a gender to each noun?

The man he'd hired from Côte d'Ivoire to teach him the ins and outs of the language had been pleasant and patient. Mostly. At the end of their sessions, Blaise wasn't the only one whose eyes had glazed over.

Possessing a fluency in the language would be more ideal than having the words translated into his lyrics and singing them. He'd thought jacking into a few lessons with a French-speaking native, watching lots of French movies with subtitles, and listening exclusively to music from Francophone African countries would help him to understand the language within months.

He'd been kidding himself. The vocabulary had been more difficult to pick up than any other language he'd learned, and he didn't sound anywhere as authentic as his teacher when he spoke.

Running barefoot under the scorching sun of his hometown while a pack of wild dogs chased him for hours on end appealed to him more than having the conversations that Armand forced him to speak in French. On a daily basis, he thought of hiding in his walk-in closet when the doorbell rang with Armand standing outside.

Blaise put a stop to the repetition of the tenses of *run*. He rummaged through the vocabulary in his brain to find the French words he needed to send the man packing for the day. Nothing but *au revoir* came to him. He'd need to say more than goodbye to keep from sounding rude.

"Let's end the session early," he said in English.

Armand flipped his wrist over and glanced at his watch. "We still have an hour and a half remaining."

Blaise rubbed his short beard, ready to throw down a lie before he realized it wasn't necessary. His tutor would still be getting paid for the whole session. "It's been a long week, and I'd like to get some rest."

It didn't take any more explanation as Armand bent his head and gathered his things. Was he grinning?

Blaise pulled out his wallet and handed Armand the money due him. Quality French lessons weren't cheap. And the way things were going with his inability to grasp onto it, they wouldn't be worth the trouble.

He limped a little from the slight throb still present in his ankle as he walked the man to the door.

"I'll see you next *Lundi*." At least, he'd gotten the word Monday correct.

Armand grimaced. "*Oui, Lundi*."

He'd pronounced the word in a one-eighty degree different way than Blaise had.

"*Lundi*," he corrected himself.

It didn't drive away the sour pucker of the man's lips. "*Au revoir*."

"*Au revoir*." He frowned at how unalike his own version had sounded to Armand's before he closed the door.

If he were any type of quitter, he'd tell his tutor to never return because he was giving up on making French the base for some of his songs with English thrown in to accentuate. Unlike other hiplife artists from Ghana, he wanted to take the Francophone countries by storm with a fresh, unique style.

The lyrics were ready; he just needed to jam the new language into them in a way that didn't make him sound like an idiot.

Blaise stumbled to the couch and flopped into it, resting this arm over his forehead. There had to be an easier way to learn. Fatigued from the mental exertion, he'd started to drift off to sleep when his cell rang.

He grunted after a quick glance at the screen. Deola. She'd been clingy over the past few weeks, her new habit of daily calls annoying. The hints she kept dropping about them taking their friendship further had thrown him off. The woman's vindictive nature wouldn't allow him to decline in a direct manner, so he'd found ways to change the subject.

There had been rumours of her shutting down a popular photography studio in Lagos when the owner decided to break up with her. He had no idea how true it was, but he wasn't willing to risk everything he'd worked so hard for by allotting her an outright rejection. He'd just have to ease her out of liking him. In the meantime, he'd continue to ignore her advances.

Other than friendship, he felt nothing for Deola. Where the woman he felt nothing for wasn't afraid to show it, the one he was drawn to her like rivers to the ocean had refused to contact him. He'd contemplated stopping by the only university in Accra that offered a doctorate program to make enquiries in the language department about his mountain woman.

Reason had kept him from making a fool of himself. Maybe she wasn't a student in the language section. Didn't she say that her dissertation had been inspired by his multilingual songs? Was she a music major?

Rather than tease himself about the possibility of stalking her, he answered the call.

"Good morning, Deola."

"Hi, Bizzy." She let out a sigh. "It took you long enough to answer. Why do you sound tired?"

He'd asked her to call him Blaise on several occasions, but she never did. "I just had a French lesson."

"I don't understand why you insist on forcing yourself to learn that language." As always, the poutiness in her tone pervaded. "If people don't speak English, that's not your fault. Besides, what do places like Benin and Côte d'Ivoire know about good music? If they had any kind of clue, your songs would be skyrocketing on their music charts." She giggled. "That's even if they have them there."

For an educated, wealthy woman who'd travelled to many countries throughout the world, she still held a limited viewpoint about, well, everything. For her, no country was as good as Nigeria. Considering they treated her as royalty there, he could somehow understand her reasoning.

He often wondered why she communicated with him. If he didn't speak Hausa like her, would she have any interest?

"For years, Côte d'Ivoire was considered to be one of the leading countries of West Africa with its advanced infrastructure and economy."

"Oh, darling." Her condescension came through loud and clear. "That was forever ago and no longer worth mentioning. Aiming to impress those people with your music is a waste of your talents. Focus on writing in English and maybe Hausa so you can catch the eye of an American artist who will be willing to collaborate with you. That's when the huge sales will come."

He definitely wouldn't shun an international collaboration. His gut told him that French lyrics would help get him there.

He ignored her unsolicited advice. "What's going on?"

"Sweetheart, does something have to be happening for us to speak? I've gotten rather addicted to our daily calls and look forward to them. You could do better by picking up the phone and ringing me every once in a while."

Her habit of manipulation infuriated him. Yet another reason they wouldn't make a functional couple. Deola needed someone she could control. He wasn't the one.

At his lack of response, she continued. "Anyway, what are you wearing to the VGMAs? It's only three weeks away. I'd like to choose a gown that matches you."

Blaise sat up straight. Had he forgotten that he'd asked her to escort him to the biggest music awards ceremony in Ghana? He raked through his memory only to come up with a no. She was continuing with their prior arrangement. If he ever wanted a real relationship to blossom with a woman he liked, he'd have to cut Deola off. Gently. Which meant with a lie.

"I hadn't planned on going."

"Don't be ridiculous." Her voice rose an octave. Quite the feat considering how high-pitched it already was. "You're up for four awards, one being Artiste of the Year. I'd like to adorn the arm of a winner. Which I know you will be."

He thought about how the tabloids would continue to splash false information about their platonic relationship. "I don't think—"

"It's okay. It's not necessary for me to know your colour. I'll wear black. It goes with everything, and I look fabulous in it. I'll be staying at Rema Resort. Same bungalow as always. Pick me up at seven. We want to make a splash with our entrance. I wouldn't be averse to you renting an upscale car. A Bentley or Jaguar will do. Get a driver, though."

She took a breath that wasn't long enough for him to get a word in.

"This is going to be so much fun. According to social media, everyone is going to be there. I'll arrange for the photographer because my posts have to be on point. My fans will expect nothing but the most glamorous pictures of us. Do you have your acceptance speech written? Don't go up there unprepared. Stumbling over your words would be beyond embarrassing. I wouldn't be able to stand it."

If he were going to get out of the date, he'd better do it now. "Listen, Deola. I appreciate the—"

"No need to thank me, babe. You're welcome. We complement each other. Beauty and talent mix perfectly together. I'll be flying into Ghana on that day because you know I don't like spending too much time in other African countries. Except for SA. I love the beachfront hotel I stay at in Cape Town. See the comfort I'm willing to sacrifice for you? By the way, in a week, I'm traveling with Daddy for two weeks onto an oil rig. He insists that I learn at least a little bit about the business. I want you to know because he told me the phone reception would be bad."

She heaved out a sigh. "Can you imagine two weeks without speaking to me? I know it will be difficult, but you'll manage. As for myself, I have no idea how I'll survive without social media. How will people be able to adore and copy my amazing fashion and style sense if they can't see me? Anyway, I'll figure it out. I always do. The stressors of my life. Not everyone would be able to handle it. Bye, honey."

The phone went dead. His breath had been stolen with it. How did he always allow her to outtalk him? Wasn't he the master of words? He had half a mind to call her back and tell her they wouldn't be attending together.

But then, who would he go with that would be comfortable with him and the paparazzi? Lamisi came to mind. The woman had been respectful, but hadn't appeared awestruck.

Time to man up. Snatching his phone from where he'd tossed it across the couch, he tapped Deola's contact.

It rang several times, and just when he was about to give up, she answered.

"Miss me already, dear?"

"Deola, I can't go with you to the VGMAs." Just like she'd done to him moments ago, he didn't give her a chance to speak. "I'm looking for a relationship, and as wonderful as you are, we aren't well-suited. I can't find someone if I'm always seen in public with you and newspapers are throwing around the rumour of us being a couple when we aren't."

He paused then to let the words sink in. "I hope you understand."

What was going through her mind? Was she planning some sort of revenge? He rolled his eyes. What could she do to his career even with her social media influence? He'd risen to the top because of his talent, not because of anything she'd done for him.

When they'd met, he'd already been well-known. That's why she'd clung to him.

She was a woman who could sense potential, and he had it in eighteen-wheeler tankards.

After the longest time, she spoke.

"You've made your feelings clear." Where was the inflection in her tone? "I thought we were going as friends. Nothing more. I understand your point. Are you seeing someone?"

"Not right now, but it's good to keep our options open just in case the right one drops into our lives."

Speaking multiple languages and being beautiful even though she doesn't have any makeup on and is sweating like three grown men.

"Are you sure? You hesitated for a moment."

There it was, the harshness in her voice that he'd anticipated.

"I'm positive. I'm flying solo these days. Working on my French and my career."

Her heavy sigh seeped into him. "I understand. Thank you for your honesty."

Did she? This wasn't the way he'd expected the conversation to go down. He'd anticipated bleeding from the ear with her screeching and yelling. Lucky for him she was being civilized.

"Good. I hope you have a safe journey on the oil rig." What else could he say? Have a great life?

"Thank you, I'll talk to you another time. Take care."

The phone went dead. Blaise stared at it for a minute before getting up and doing part of the choreographed dances for one of his songs.

He'd dodged a bullet. From what he'd heard, no one told her no, but he'd gotten away with it.

More dancing.

Now, to find that special woman who sparked his soul. Someone he'd want to spend the rest of his life with. Had he already met her and let her go without even trying?

CHAPTER TEN

Lamisi procrastinated calling Blaise after the meeting with her horror of a supervisor by completing the interview questions he'd requested. Then she'd researched and compiled a list of Ghanaian hiplife artists who would suit her project if they were available. Her hips were loose and flexible from all the dancing she'd done while listening to their music.

When that task had been completed, her parent's house, where she would continue to live until she received her doctorate or got married—whichever came first—absolutely had to be cleaned from top to bottom. It didn't matter that they had a cleaner come in once a week to do that task.

Exhausted, she showered and lay on her bed. Maybe seven at night was too late to call him.

She scoffed at her own state of ridiculousness.

What if he refused to help her? Even worse, hung up?

Nerves rattling enough to make her stomach squeamish and her mouth so dry that she didn't think she'd be able to speak if he did answer, she stared at his number for the billionth time. Good things never came to those who didn't try, so she squeezed her eyes shut and touched an index finger to where the blue phone icon should be.

The phone flew away from her ear when a voice said, "Hello," on the third ring.

She caught her cell with the opposite hand before it could slam onto the floor, breaking yet another protective glass cover.

"Hello?" Definitely Blaise's entrancing voice.

"Um, hi. This is …" She placed a hand on her chest in an attempt to calm her palpitating heart and took a quick breath. Professionalism was the key. She was calling him for help with her dissertation, not to ask him out. If he said no, she'd find someone else. Simple as that. "Hello Blaise, this is Lamisi Imoro."

His turn to go silent. Maybe he had no recollection of her.

"We met climbing Mt. Afadjato a few weeks ago. I understood when your friends were speaking in Hausa. We drove you home when you sprained your ankle. My friend, Precious, told you that I'm your biggest fan."

Shut up already! How many other people had he met on that mountain?

"Yes. I remember."

His emotionless tone told her he no longer had an interest in her. Why did that fill her with so much disappointment?

"Good. How are you? And how's your ankle?"

"I'm well and on the mend. Not at a hundred percent yet, but much better. Thanks for asking. What's going on?"

She wiped away the sweat dripping onto her phone as she held in her standard reply of being fine herself. He hadn't asked of her welfare in return. May as well get it over with.

"I'm working on my dissertation for my PhD."

"I recall that I was your inspiration for the topic."

She heard the smile in his voice, and her tight muscles relaxed in response. "You were. I met with my supervisor, and he suggested that I add interviews from a few multi-lingual artists."

"You'd like to interview me," he said without any type of inflection to let her know how he felt about it.

"If you could make time in your schedule for me to ask you some questions, I'd really appreciate it."

The line remained silent. The whooshing of blood through her arteries filled her ears as she angled her body forward, hoping he'd say yes.

"I'd also venture to guess that you'd like me to get in contact with some of my colleagues to arrange interviews with them."

She didn't miss that he had neither accepted nor declined the interview.

"Actually, that would be very helpful." She hated being on the receiving end of a favour.

"I'll do the interview."

She let out a sigh of relief. "Thank you. Anything you can do about getting me some artists that are almost as great as you?"

"Good one," he said with a chuckle. "I'll see what I can do. How about if we get together and discuss it in person?"

They'd be meeting for research purposes, she reminded herself as she tugged on one of her twists and chewed the corner of her bottom lip. It wasn't a date. Not even close.

"Sure," she said with a casualness that made her proud. "When are you available?"

"I have a meeting in the morning, so how about in the afternoon?"

"Tomorrow?"

Where was the time she'd need to mentally prepare herself for seeing him again? Her body needed strong warnings to keep from reacting to him.

"If you're available." Was that hesitation in his voice? "It would be best to schedule with the other artists as soon as possible."

He was right. She'd just have to get over herself and put her education at the forefront. Unsolicited physical responses to Blaise be damned.

"Tomorrow afternoon would be fine. Where should we meet and what time?"

"I'll be in Accra. Where do you live? I could pick you up."

And have it feel like a date? No way. Her heart wouldn't be able to take it, and her mind would lose the necessary focus to get through the encounter with him. She'd spend the time zoning out that he'd said he liked her rather than concentrating on her project.

Who was she kidding? That would probably happen anyway while looking at him. His eyes were hypnotic with their intensity. And his lips. Full, dark, and soft. Irresistible.

"Hello? Lamisi? Are you still there?"

"Hello, can you hear me?" She played into the consistent network problems that plagued the phone network systems. "Hello?"

"I can hear you," Blaise said. "Can you hear me?"

"Yes. I live in East Legon. I could meet you at Cool It in Legon Mall." The place wasn't as crowded as the bigger restaurant in Accra, so she wouldn't have to watch throngs of his fans snatch his attention.

"I don't mind picking you up. I'll be at Circle."

"That's okay. I have an appointment with my supervisor in the morning, so I'll be in the area of the mall. What time?"

"How about at one?"

Professor Amartey should be done berating her research skills long before then. "Sounds good."

"Okay, I'll see you at one."

Tempering down her squeal, she kept her voice level. "Okay. Bye."

"Bye." He sang rather than spoke, bringing a huge smile to her face.

She pressed the end call button and sighed. Not only would she see him again, but he'd agreed to help her. If she hadn't had a major crush on him before, it would've started right that minute. Something she had to guard against now that he was involved in her research.

She couldn't afford to have her doctorate disapproved because of bias due to a personal relationship with one of the interviewees. Not after everything she'd gone through to get to that point.

***

Blaise finished his second drink of ginger beer within the hour he'd been waiting at the restaurant for Lamisi. She'd sent a text saying she was running late.

When had he last waited an hour for someone? It tended to be the other way around. At least, she hadn't cancelled. She'd only called for a favour, not because she liked him. And yet, he got the sense that she did.

He hadn't gotten jittery at hearing a woman's voice in a very long time. He'd wanted to keep her on the phone last night, chatting about nothing and everything.

What was it about her that he found so special? He could find beauty, charm, and intelligence in so many women in Ghana. Lamisi possessed a quality he had yet to identify that had caught and kept his attention when others hadn't. Probably why he was still lingering around with his stomach growling when he could've eaten and left.

The door to the Jamaican restaurant opened. His breath caught when Lamisi stepped in and looked around the place. Finding him, she walked towards his corner table. He slid out of the booth as she reached him.

Wearing a light green, button-down dress shirt tucked into a navy-blue straight skirt, she got into the booth. "I'm so sorry to have kept you waiting."

"That's okay." Glad to finally be together after two weeks of missing her, he smiled. "At least you called. More than I've gotten from others."

She shook her head. "I hate wasting people's time. It's just that my supervisor held me up."

Her eyes started glistening. If that wasn't enough to concern him, her sniffles were. "What's wrong?"

She fanned a hand in front of her face.

"Nothing. I'm just ..." She swallowed hard before pointing to his glass. "May I?"

Not waiting for an answer, she reached for the water and took several sips. It didn't seem to help as the tears escaped her eyes and trailed down her cheeks.

The bench squeaked as he shifted closer to her. His fist clenched with the urge to eradicate whatever or whoever had upset her.

"Lamisi, what's wrong?"

Taking a tissue, she swiped her face with a force that left him surprised she hadn't caused herself injury.

"My supervisor is such an arrogant know-it-all ass." Her eyes kept filling. "He makes me so angry, I could punch him."

She banged the bottom of her fist against the table, making the glasses shake.

He waited for the reason behind the tears. Minutes passed with her silence. "Why are you crying?"

"I told you, I'm upset at my supervisor's behaviour." She sniffed and drank more of his water. "From the first moment I got assigned to him, he's given me a hard time. He's the kind of professor that wants to be the only one at the top of the pyramid. He makes things difficult so I'll want to give up on attaining my doctorate."

He had to be missing something. "And?"

"I'm not going to quit." She blew her nose. "I've come too far."

The tears had stopped, leaving her eyes red and him still not understanding. "Did he make you sad?"

"No. Why?"

He'd never had a more confusing conversation in his life. "Because you were crying."

She stared at him with her brows drawn as if she were the one confused. And then, as if comprehension dawned, she laughed. She couldn't seem to stop. He'd missed the sound as much as he had her.

"Thanks, Blaise. I needed that."

"You're welcome?" He could accept gratitude even though he had no idea what he'd done.

"It's embarrassing, but I cry when I'm exasperated." She shrugged. "I guess it's better than throwing things, but people end up thinking that I'm sensitive."

"You aren't."

She rolled her eyes. "Not at all. I'm pretty sure that if I didn't cry when I got angry, I'd end up in jail for beating someone, or at least trying. It's as if God infused me with that annoying trait to save His people from my wrath."

Intriguing. "Then what do you do when you're sad?"

"Cry. But it's different."

"Okay."

She looked him in the eyes.

"I'm sorry. I didn't mean for you to see me like that. I've held it in for too long. My supervisor would've never let me live it down if I had cried in front of him." She stuck her tongue out and looked down at it. "I thought I'd bitten it so hard that it might be swollen."

He chuckled, still not clear about what had just happened, but glad to have the lighter version of Lamisi back.

The server came over. "Are you ready to order?"

Without looking at the menu, Lamisi said, "I'll have oxtail with beans and rice, and a glass of ginger beer."

"Curried chicken and plain rice," Blaise said.

"Anything to drink?"

"A big bottle of water."

The server left with a nod.

"Why don't you get a new supervisor if this one is frustrating you?"

The sound she made lay somewhere between a whimper and a grunt. "He's my third. My first supervisor was amazing. Just before the end of my third year, he died."

Blaise hoped he didn't set her off with the depressing conversation. "Sorry to hear that."

"Me, too." Lamisi smiled. "Professor Ogah had a great influence on how I viewed linguistics. He spoke more languages than I did and gave me a better understanding of how I learned. He changed my life and way of thinking about languages." Her shoulders slumped. "He's in a better place now."

"Yes." What else could he say?

"Long story short, my second supervisor moved to another country, and then the third one in line, Professor Amartey, took her place." She said the name with teeth exposed in a snarl. "He makes writing my dissertation a living Hell."

The muscle in his jaw ticked as rage at the injustice Lamisi had faced brought out a growl. "That's not right. Do you need me to talk to him to ease up?"

Her head flinched back.

Had he said something wrong?

"No, but thanks. I can handle my own battles. He hasn't crossed any type of line into abuse or anything like that. He just doesn't appreciate how much work I've been applying to the dissertation and is highly critical about everything I turn in. Including the interview questions for the artists I submitted. He had me wait for two hours in his office while he attended a meeting before he gave me his suggestions."

Not ready to stand down with his offer, he leaned in. "Let me know if anything changes. I can be quite influential."

She nodded and grinned. "I can handle it myself. Thanks for the offer."

His heart expanded at the sweetness of her smile, making him feel even more protective of her. Blaise held his index finger and thumb a centimetre apart. "Just a little chat with him? He'll be as kind as a puppy to you afterwards."

Her incredible brown eyes twinkled. "As much as I'd like my supervisor to be docile, I decline."

His head and shoulders slumped with the drama of his heaved grunt of a sigh. "Okay. Fine."

Little did she know that the next time her supervisor made her cry, for whatever reason, he'd be in the guy's office so fast that plaster would fly off of the walls.

She deserved to be treated well. By everyone.

How had he come to care so much about a woman he had only recently met?

There was only one answer. The same thing that had kept him thinking about her. She was different. He'd be an idiot to not realize it. An even bigger fool to let her slip away from him again.

CHAPTER ELEVEN

Having skipped breakfast due to fear of vomiting in her stress-inducing supervisor's office, Lamisi downed her oxtail and rice as if it had been a week rather than all night since she'd last eaten.

The whole episode of her fury-induced breakdown in front of Blaise had more entertained rather than humiliated her.

She'd found the fact that he'd offered himself as her protector to be both horrifying because he didn't see her as someone who could take care of her own problems, and sweet because it showed that he cared. The man had a way of chipping away the resistance she'd built against him.

She took a break from her food and glanced around at the full restaurant. "I'm surprised no one recognized you."

He tipped his head towards one of the tables across the room. She twisted her torso to observe a group of women stealing covert glances in his direction and whispering to themselves.

"They aren't sure if I'm who they think I am. I rarely get approached when I'm out. For those bold enough to do so, I appease them with a conversation, sometimes a photo."

She shook her head. "That's not how I imagined your public life to be. I thought it would be more like we see on television."

"Very few Ghanaians have a reaction to me one way or the other. They're too busy trying to find their own way through life to worry about me. You're my number one fan, and yet, you ignored me when we first met."

"That's not true. I smiled and winked back."

"Ah, yes," he said in that breathy voice that made her shiver. "That moment is imprinted in my mind forever. Just as I was about to approach you, your face went all sour."

She laughed when he scrunched his features together and sucked his cheeks in.

"I wasn't that bad."

She bowed her head for a second before facing him with the truth.

"I didn't know how to handle your attention." Starting with his head, her hand waved to where his torso met the table. "You're a handsome musician with successful albums to your name, and I'm ... me. The encounter wasn't what I expected."

Hinging at the hips, he leaned closer, propped his elbows on the table, and gave her a lopsided flash of teeth that made her want to crawl over the barrier to close the space between them.

"You think I'm handsome?"

An eye-roll accompanied her drawn-out teeth sucking. The man knew his appeal, so his joke fell flat.

"How about we discuss the interviews I need for my research?"

She reached into her bag and pulled out a printed sheet of paper which included the title of her project, its objectives, and the names of the top fifteen Ghanaian multilingual hiplife artists who best suited the parameters of her dissertation.

Blaise was number one. Professor Amartey had agreed to the list of artists. She got the sense it was because he didn't know who they were; otherwise, things may have gone in a more harrowing direction.

The server came to remove their plates and asked if they wanted dessert. They both declined.

Blaise read through the list. "Ambitious, aren't you?"

She shrugged. "Since I already knew the greatest of the greats, I figured you'd have no difficulty hooking me up with at least seven of the others."

"Slick. When would you like to conduct the interviews?"

"Since my supervisor has approved the interview questions, anytime this week or next would be perfect. Each interview will take about an hour, and I can meet them anywhere they want."

"Can I be with you for the interviews?"

She kept her face from morphing into a look of surprise at his request. Why would he want to be?

"Between travelling and the interview itself, that would take up a lot of your time, which I'm sure you could spend on more worthwhile ventures, like writing fabulous chart-climbing songs."

She hoped she'd been diplomatic enough for his ego.

"Besides, your presence might skew the artist's answers, which wouldn't provide a true evaluation for my research."

"In that case." He picked up the pen she'd placed on the table. "Is it okay if I write on this?"

"Yes."

Blaise struck out two of the names on the list.

"Why did you do that?"

He tapped the pen between the two names he'd cancelled out. "I wouldn't trust these guys alone with a beautiful woman. So, I won't even ask them."

Heat crept up her neck and resided in her cheeks. With all the women he must encounter, he thought her beautiful? Would she sound as if she were begging for a compliment if she asked him to repeat himself?

For the next forty minutes, Lamisi watched him contact his musician colleagues. His ability to smooth-talk them into accepting to do the interview had her mesmerized. If she could speak to people like that, she'd probably want for nothing ever again.

Eight confirmations had her clapping and kicking her legs under the table with excitement.

"Thank you so much, Blaise. I'll be a busy woman this week with interviews every day until Friday, but it'll be worth it. *And* I get to meet some of the best hiplife artists in Ghana. Thank you. Thank you. Thank you. What can I do to repay you?"

He rubbed his chin. "Well, there is one thing."

"Name it."

"Can you help me to learn French?"

Not what she'd been expecting. Their conversation on the mountain came back to her. "You said you wanted to use it in your next album. Haven't you started to learn?"

He tugged at his ear, something she'd never noticed him do before.

"I have a tutor, but it's not going very well. I thought I was good with languages, but French seems to be the exception. Those tenses are impossible to learn."

"Wouldn't my teaching you be the same as the tutor that you already have?"

"Not exactly."

She had so much to do to get her dissertation written and ready to defend against a panel that would tear her apart if she didn't complete the work well. She'd taken a one-year leave of absence from her job as an assistant lecturer at the university, but she didn't want to squander her time by becoming a private tutor when she could be writing her research.

Yet, she owed him. Big time. Saying no would be rude, but she had to think of herself first. Didn't she?

***

Lamisi's excitement from only moments ago had decelerated when he'd presented his request.

The idea had bounced into his brain that he'd have a more enjoyable time learning the language if she were to teach him.

"What do you mean, not exactly?" she asked. "A tutor is a tutor. When you do the work, you get the results."

The woman was tough. He needed that if he were to reach his goal.

"Believe me, I've been studying all the time, but something's missing." *You.* "I'll be going into the studio to start recording in about six weeks, and so far, my lyrics are still all in English."

Since he'd been having such a hard time with French, and Lamisi didn't seem keen on helping him to learn, he needed to take a different tack. "How about rather than me trying to learn the language in that time, which would be impossible, you help me translate some of it?"

He'd thought about just doing a translation before, but knew that being fluent in the language would make him sound better while singing it. This way, as she translated the lyrics, he could learn the language from a more practical level.

She looked at him from the corner of her eye. "Why can't your tutor interpret for you?"

When was the last time he'd faced so much resistance from someone? People tended to fall at his feet wanting to make him happy. He appreciated Lamisi's style of staying true to herself. A respectable quality that mirrored him. How much more did they have in common?

"Let's just say that Gospel is more his style of music. I don't think he's ever listened to a secular song. If I asked him, he'd probably clasp a hand against his chest, raise the other one while bowing his head, and exclaim, 'Jesus take the wheel!'"

Her laughter held the same huskiness of her voice, pleasing his ears. He needed more.

"My tutor would exclaim it in French, and he'd add backward hops to emphasize his point."

"Oh … my … goodness," she said between her guffaws and smacking the table. "Stop it. I can totally see it."

He chuckled. "I haven't described him, so someone in your life must have left a strong impression."

Her laughter ended with a sigh. "Definitely."

"What he's teaching me is practical for if I travel. When will I ever sing about asking where the toilet is? Can you see why he's out of the running for lyrics translator?"

Getting her to agree was paramount, so he rushed on with his argument. "He may be technically knowledgeable about the language, but I don't hear a flow in him."

Her head dipped to the side as an indent formed in the middle of her forehead. "A flow?"

Blaise nodded and undulated his arm in a wave-like motion. "The tempo that will translate in the music so it doesn't sound straight or stilted."

"You've lost me."

He rummaged for a term she'd relate to? "He's monotonous."

"No up or down rhythm in his speech." Her head bobbed. "I get it now."

Not everyone did. "You possess the flow, and it will help me to decide which lyrics should be sung in French and which should be in English. And ..."

He paused to pique her interest.

Her eyes widened. "What?"

"Who would be better to help me create my first French/English album than my number one fan?"

She burst into laughter. "Damn, you're good."

He thought so. "Does that mean you'll help me?"

"How long do you think it would take to do the translations?"

At least, it wasn't a no. "It's only for six songs. I can't see it taking more than a couple of days."

She rotated the empty glass which had contained her water while she thought.

"Please say you'll help to make me the king of French/English hiplife."

"Considering that hiplife is based in Ghana, it's doubtful. You may need to go with the term they use in Francophone countries for similar music. Closer to zouglou, zouk, or Coupé-Décalé. Have you decided which style you'll sing in?"

His jaw dropped. "You're one impressive woman."

She plucked at her shirt. "I sure am."

He chuckled. "I've got the musical styling covered. We'll discuss it if you decide to help me with the translation."

"Since I owe you and it won't take too much of my time. Okay."

Blaise pumped a fist in the air.

"How about this weekend so we can get it out of the way?" she asked in a dry tone.

"Your enthusiasm is contagious," he teased.

"Sorry, but I'm very busy," she said with one side of her mouth quirked upward in a partial smile.

"Working on albums that will expand the scope of music in Africa, maybe the world as we now know it, is not my main priority."

His chest swelled with the confidence she had in him. "I see. I won't take it personally then, Dr. Imoro-to-be."

A full smile bloomed on her face, raising his spirits even higher.

He shifted closer to her as his gaze fell to her lips before rising to her eyes. "How about we seal the deal?"

Her mouth rounded. "Oh?"

He descended his head slowly to give her the opportunity to decline. Her lids hovering at the closing point encouraged him on.

The brush of their lips caused a shock to travel through him, just as it had on the mountain. He'd anticipated this moment since she'd stormed into the restaurant. No—since they'd last seen each other.

He moaned when she raised a hand to his jaw as their lips merged.

Drenched in her scent of sweet roses, his greatest desire was to deepen the kiss. He did the gentlemanly thing and backed away. They were in a public place, even though most of the lunchtime diners had cleared out.

He stared into her eyes with her hand still moulded against his cheek.

"Sealed with a kiss," he said once his mind had cleared enough for words to form.

He knew without a doubt that he'd turn it into a song one day and dedicate it to her.

CHAPTER TWELVE

Three of the most incredible days of Lamisi's life had gone by in a whirlwind of heart-racing excitement. How many times had she pinched herself when in the midst of such extraordinary Ghanaian musicians? They had all been gracious and generous with their time and answers. A few of them had even wanted her to contact them about the results of the research, which had elevated her exhilaration into the outer galaxies.

Other than receiving several calls from an unknown number with someone breathing on the other end of the line without speaking, it had been a perfect week.

She'd gotten Blaise's interview out of the way first. After the ease of conversing with him about his music, she'd found the interactions with the others to be more of a comfortable chat than a strict interview.

She smiled when Blaise answered his phone on Friday. For the past few days, she had called and gushed her gratitude for having set her up with the artists. They'd end up talking about their day, which she enjoyed. Talking to him was like conversing with a friend who had the ability to make her core pulse with a need that hadn't been fulfilled in a very long time.

"Lamisi, if you thank me one more time, I'm going to turn each of the interviews you did into their own favour."

The giggle tripped out of her. "Okay. Okay. No more. How was your day?"

"Stressful."

She sat up in the seat at her desk, ready to take care of whatever had worried him. "Why? What happened?"

"My manager wants a few of the new songs ready by the VGMAs."

Lamisi watched the most popular music awards held in Ghana every year. "When are they holding them?"

"In three weeks. They asked me to perform. As my manager pointed out, it would be the perfect platform to introduce the new sound."

It certainly would since the ceremony was broadcast all over West Africa. "Can you have them ready by then?"

"Yes. The tunes and the lyrics are set. At least the English version. I just need my star translator to transition them into French. Are we still on for tomorrow?"

After having his voice in her ear all week, nothing could keep her from seeing him again. "Yes."

"Great. I can pick you up and bring you to my place."

A loud 'no' resonated in her head. She couldn't be alone with him in his home. She'd kissed him in a restaurant and had longed for more. What would her traitorous body allow him to do if they were alone? They hadn't known each other long enough. "Can't we meet somewhere more public?"

"I have recording equipment in my home that we'll be using."

"Oh."

"How about if you bring someone with you? As long as they don't tell the world about my project, it'll be fine."

Had he read her mind, or had she been so conservative in her dealings with him that he'd guessed why she'd hesitated? A smile spread across her face at his ability to make her feel at ease.

Tomorrow being Saturday, she could ask any number of people to join her. Her youngest brother Amadu had completed his exams; he'd be perfect. Precious had a wedding to attend—otherwise, she'd have been her first choice. "Okay. What time?"

"I'm under a bit of pressure to get this completed. How about eight? We'll get some work done, and then, I'll feed you lunch."

"Sounds like a deal. See you then. Can you send me the address?"

"Will do. Have a good night."

"You, too."

Just like every time she'd spoken to him, she hung up first. Lingering on the phone would be too telling of how much she liked him.

Whether anything would come of it, only time would tell.

CHAPTER THIRTEEN

Lamisi parked in front of Blaise's estate house and got out of the car. Two doors clicked closed before hers. Amadu had jumped at the opportunity to meet Bizzy, and so had Precious when she'd mentioned it.

"I'm going with you. It's only a wedding I'm missing out on," Precious had said. "Besides, I barely speak to my colleague. She won't even know I'm not there. I can't miss an opportunity to experience musical history in the making."

Lamisi hadn't been able to talk her friend out of joining them. So instead of one guardian at her side, she was flanked by two, both much too excited about hanging out at Blaise's place.

The front door opened before they reached it. He'd known they'd arrived in the estate complex when they'd needed his permission to clear security at the front gate.

Blaise stepped out of his home wearing a pair of well-worn jeans with a yellow T-shirt that outlined his muscular chest and arms. The strength of his body stayed imprinted on her own. The consistent memory of the gentle brush of his soft lips still stirred butterflies in her stomach.

Lamisi's mouth went dry at the sight of him. His beard remained trimmed and his hair was the same low-cut style it had been when she'd last seen him a few days ago. Yet, his handsomeness had quadrupled. If such a thing could be tallied.

"Welcome."

The moment he opened his arms out to her, she skipped forward to ensconce herself into them. The sun blazing down on them had nothing on the heat her body absorbed when she looped her arms around his waist and melted from chest to thigh into his solid strength.

She closed her eyes and clung tighter to his perfect form as her body buzzed with an awareness that curled her toes. Her senses overloaded with his presence as his unique smell wafted into her nose. A mix of … She took a deep whiff to discern the scent. Leather and citrus. She could get drunk from the combination.

He released her before she was anywhere near ready.

The hug with Precious wasn't as intimate or long as the one they'd shared. Her insides danced at that.

"Hello, Precious. How have you been?"

"Hi, Blaise. Life's been busy, but good. How's the ankle?"

"Mostly healed. Every once in a while, I get a twinge of pain, but it's manageable."

Lamisi introduced the men.

A clap of hands introduced their handshake before their palms slid along each other, ending in a snap of their fingers.

Blaise's lips rose with a smile. "Good to meet you, Amadu."

Her protective little brother displayed a polite reserve which was unlike his bold personality. "You, too. I'm a big fan of your music."

A huge understatement.

"So far, it sounds like I have a solid fan base in the Imoro family."

"Not everyone, man." Amadu's honest nature came to the forefront, as usual. "My father won't listen to anything but old school high life, and my eldest sister is Gospel all the way. The rest of us, even my mother, are more eclectic in our music tastes."

Blaise glanced at her with a brow raised and a twinkle in his eyes. "Gospel, you say?"

Lamisi giggled at their inside joke.

"Nothing but," Amadu responded with a curious look at Lamisi.

He led them into his home.

"Oh, my goodness," Precious whispered with more than a touch of awe.

Lamisi whole-heartedly agreed as the air-conditioned atmosphere hit her. Dark brown leather couches and chairs cradling light yellow and orange throw pillows filled the perimeter of the living area. The tan and white rug below the coffee table met the edges of the seats. A plasma screen television took up a third of the opposite wall.

The rust colour of two walls gave the room a warm glow while the light grey in the dining area and the barrier which held the door they'd just entered appeared to expand it.

He'd given the space a Ghanaian feel with a few carved wood masks and vivid paintings of scenery of their homeland.

"Make yourselves at home," Blaise said. "I'll be right back."

They settled side by side onto the couch. Lamisi held back a groan as she ran a hand against the buttery soft material while being enveloped in a seat with the perfect amount of firmness and sinkability.

Amadu hadn't stopped gawping at the flat screen. "This place is inspiration."

"Is it just me, or is the house massive?" Lamisi asked.

"I wouldn't have guessed how far it extended. And this is just the living and dining room." Precious pointed towards the staircase. "Did either of you notice a second floor from the outside?"

"No. I thought it was a single story." Then again, she'd been too busy basking in Blaise's embrace to notice much of anything other than him.

Amadu twisted his upper body. "Is that a swimming pool in the back?"

They stood as if attached by a wire and looked out of the windows protected by an intricately designed metallic burglar-proofing system. A gleaming, crystal clear in-ground swimming pool met her gaze.

"I don't see a wall enclosure. How big do you think the property is?" Precious asked.

"It's six plots," Blaise announced as he came into the room with a tray of bottled water.

Never in seven lifetimes would she have guessed that he'd be the one to serve them. Didn't he have a house help? He couldn't maintain this incredible home by himself. Could he?

Out of habit, she stepped forward to take the tray from him.

"Please sit. You're my guest."

She sank into the seat, once again impressed by him.

They each plucked a bottle of water from the tray with a word of thanks.

Blaise sat in an armchair. "How about a tour of the grounds before we start work?"

"If it isn't an inconvenience." Lamisi kept her voice light instead of letting the eagerness come through.

"Not at all."

They formed a queue behind him as if on a school excursion.

He swung right when they reached the dining room into a kitchen that made Lamisi's knees weaken with envy.

Light brown wood cabinets broke the cream-coloured theme of the walls and marble-looking countertops.

He reached for one of the tall cabinet handles and opened it to reveal a full refrigerator. She'd only seen such a beautifully hidden panel on television shows.

Saliva filled her mouth at the eight-burner stainless steel range making up part of the centre island.

"Do you enjoy cooking?" Precious asked.

"Yes, but for the most part, I leave the task to my Aunt Vida who prepares my meals. She's amazing."

Lamisi raised a brow at Precious when Blaise turned his back. A man who knew how to cook and openly admitted it. Intriguing.

They walked to the far side of the home past the swimming pool, guest house, and a massive garden. A shelter housed two vehicles and a motorcycle.

Lamisi's body thrummed with memories of rides that had left her invigorated. Her hands had gripped the handles as the motorcycle vibrated beneath her. The engine had revved with the hum of a lion as she'd taken to the road, owning it. It had been much too long since she'd controlled the kind of power that left her feeling free and uninhibited.

As if hypnotized, she ambled over to the red and black Suzuki and stroked the sleek machine from its cool metallic handle bars to its elevated seat which would sink as soon as her ass sat on it. Such a fine vehicle. Could anyone else hear it begging her to straddle it and show it love by taking it out for a spin? She raised her leg to obey.

"If you don't get her away from that motorcycle—" Amadu warned, "—you'll never get your translations done."

Lamisi's foot hit the ground as she looked up from her trance to find Blaise standing next to her.

He stepped closer. "You're kidding, right?"

Amadu shook his head. "Not even a little. She learned how to ride one when we visited our family in the north."

"Makes sense," Blaise said. "Considering that it's a common mode of transportation along with bicycles."

"She kind of got obsessed with the speed aspect." Amadu rubbed a hand over his head. "Turned my parents prematurely grey when she flew by their car one day. As much as she pleaded for one when we returned to Accra, they refused."

Lamisi waved her hand in her brother's face. "Hey. I'm right here. That was a long time ago, Amadu. I've gotten over it."

Mostly. She wouldn't brag about having gotten a motorcycle license and borrowing one of her friend's bikes every once in a while. The exhilaration of the wind rushing past never got old.

Precious grunted. "Once a speed demon, always …"

She let the rest of her words hang.

Lamisi took one last, longing glance at the motorcycle that would feature in her dreams tonight. She looked up at Blaise who seemed to be considering her. Too bad mind-reader wasn't on her list of talents.

By the time they'd finished seeing the house, she had lost Amadu to the video game collection and Precious to the gym. At least, they wouldn't be too far away in the unique basement space.

Her jaw dropped when they encountered the mini studio he'd spoken of.

"This is not small, Blaise," she accused while taking in the hardwood floors, a closed-in booth with clear glass or plastic—she couldn't tell—and equipment she'd only seen on shows or movies about music.

"Compared to professional recording studios, it is."

Lamisi touched the panelled wall. "Is it sound-proof?"

"Yes. If I were hard-pressed, I could create an album here, but I use the place to tinker around and get my creative juices flowing. I leave the work of blending to my producer since he's so good at it."

Where was the cockiness she'd expected from someone who'd made it big in such a competitive business? Maybe they weren't as different as she'd initially thought.

CHAPTER FOURTEEN

Blaise refused to let liking Lamisi get in the way of business. He'd handed her a non-disclosure agreement before exposing her to his work. The pain of past betrayals had served as a lesson. She didn't seem to mind as she scrolled her signature onto the form after listening to his reasoning for it and then reading it.

They settled into the seats at the desktop computers he'd set up in his studio. Keeping his hands to himself during their session would be a feat of Mt. Afadjato proportions so he'd left the door open as an added incentive to behave.

She hadn't exposed her breasts or legs in the overkill manner other women used to catch his attention, yet her jeans and loose-fitting red dashiki top tempted. Her hair had been freshly twisted and framed her face. Unlike the day they had met on the mountain and the restaurant, she wore makeup that enhanced her beauty. Especially her exotic, angular eyes. Breath-taking.

In the past few moments alone, he'd sucked in discrete deep breaths to take in more of her sweet yet somehow spicy rose fragrance. He'd have to set his mind to concentration mode in order to get the work done.

"I have six songs I'd like to translate."

"Will they be the only ones on the album?"

He clicked a folder on the desktop.

"No, but those are the ones which will be mixed with French. If I can pull it off," he mumbled the last.

Her hand on his shoulder sent a simmering buzz into him. When would he get used to the fact that their attraction was inevitable and electric?

"You can do it," she assured. "To the best of my knowledge, it's never been done on such a grand level by a Ghanaian artist, but if anyone can pull it off, you can."

His chest puffed out with pride at her confidence in him. Support was a treasurable thing. The fact that she gave it out so freely and believed in him said a lot about the kindness and generosity of her personality.

He clicked on the song he'd entitled 'You're the One for Me.'

Lamisi scanned the words that popped up on the page. "How's this going to work?"

"You asked me about the style of the songs." He clicked on the bottom of the screen and opened his music player. His voice came through the speakers singing the English lyrics to the song he'd set to a rough beat he'd created.

Lamisi bopped her head and shook her shoulders. A good sign.

She crossed her arms over her chest and sighed when the song finished.

"Oh my goodness, those lyrics are beautiful. You've combined hiplife with zouglou." She grabbed his forearm with her eyes wide. "Blaise, you've created a whole new style of music. That's so incredible."

He blinked at her several times. Not for the first time, he wondered about the incredible woman sitting next to him. "I'm impressed. You really know your music styles."

She tucked her hair behind her ear and avoided his gaze by staring at the computer screen. "I'm a fan of all genres of music. Like languages, I recognize them easily."

The woman wore modesty like a light jacket during the cool dry Harmattan season. She possessed gifts that would make most people walk around with their nose stuck in the air looking down on everyone who didn't come up to her level.

How much more would he discover about her that would astonish him?

Rather than embarrass her further, he got to work. "Which of the lyrics will flow well in French to the beat?"

Time to see if he'd made the right choice with her, at least when it came to his career. Their personal relationship would be determined later.

***

Lamisi startled at the knock on the door.

A woman about the same age as her mother stood with her hands clenched together. "I'm sorry to disturb, but lunch has been ready for over two hours. Amadu and Precious have already eaten."

Lamisi extended her body in a stretch that loosened tight muscles. "What time is it?"

Blaise displayed the face of his watch by flipping his wrist over. "Two o'clock."

Grabbing his hand, she twisted his arm with disbelief to look for herself. "We've been at this for five hours?"

"It would appear that way." He rotated his chair towards the door. "We'll be up in a minute, Aunty. Thank you for coming to get us."

The older woman's smile pulled out a dimple on each of her chubby cheeks. "I know how you can go all day without eating when you're in here. It's not good for the body to work without sustenance."

Not waiting for a reply, she turned and left.

"Five hours?" Lamisi still couldn't understand how so much time had passed.

His laughter didn't diminish her incredulity. When had she ever done anything where time flew by so fast? Sleeping didn't count.

Focusing on the task had been impossible at first with her heart racing at his nearness. The occasional brush of knees when they swivelled their seats in the same direction happened too often to be coincidence.

And then, the job at hand had taken over, and that's when everything but translating the lyrics had possessed them.

Getting to her feet, she tipped her neck from side to side, and then rolled it around. "This happens to you a lot?"

He towered over her when he unfolded himself from the chair. "It does. Losing myself in the music is what makes me so good."

She bumped his shoulder with her fist. "Here I was, thinking you were humble."

Hands crossed over his chest as he arched backwards, he widened his eyes and gasped. "Who, me?"

"I don't remember you being half as dramatic during your shows as you are in real life."

"That's because my manager said I had to tone it down."

Their combined laughter filled the studio. No longer jittery about being near him, she could definitely get used to hanging out.

She may not get the chance again because they only had two songs left to translate. Now that they'd developed a rhythm, it shouldn't take long. Would they remain friends? She'd really like that.

Who was she kidding? She wanted more.

She placed a hand over her stomach when it rumbled.

"Sounds like I overworked you. Let's go eat."

She followed him out of the secure haven she'd discovered in the studio. Would working on her dissertation in this room make time fly? She doubted it. The combination of being with such a talented man while creating something new and inventive had to be a contributing factor.

They walked in on Amadu fixated on a football video game in the entertainment room and left him to it.

Now, she prayed that Precious would also be occupied so she'd have Blaise all to herself for a little while longer.

CHAPTER FIFTEEN

It didn't take ten minutes for Lamisi to empty her bowl of the eba and okra soup. She sighed in contentment as she rested against the seat. "Please don't tell my mom, but that was the best okra soup I've ever eaten in my life."

The eba, as they called it in Nigeria, made from gari, a dried and then fried cassava, had been mixed with hot water to give it a more solid yet sticky consistency for shaping and scooping out the stew-like soup by hand. She hadn't been embarrassed to lick her fingers once the food had disappeared.

Blaise placed a single finger over his lips. "Your secret is safe with me."

"What do you do when your mother comes to visit?"

"I warn Aunty Vida not to cook as well."

The older woman laughed as she came to the table. "As if I could downplay the gift Allah has graced me with. Besides, my cousin comes to visit just to eat from my hand. Would you like some more food? There's plenty."

She struggled to sit up from her lounged position in order to show respect. "No, thank you, Aunty Vida. It was absolutely delicious, but I'm full."

She was even too replete to hide the slight bulge that made an appearance over the waistline of her jeans. If she were home, she'd unbutton them, but in Blaise's house, she brought her chair closer to the table, hoping he wouldn't notice.

The woman picked up their bowls before Lamisi could offer to help and swooshed out of the room whistling a happy tune.

Eating a Ghanaian woman's food and then complaining about how stuffed you were tended to bring out all sorts of joy.

"She's your aunt by blood?" she half-whispered.

"Yes." He kept his voice as low as hers. "Not only is she my cook, but she's my parents' spy."

"Interesting."

"More like annoying. But my parents didn't want someone they didn't know preparing my meals. Being a chief, my dad can get paranoid. The good thing is that she doesn't stay in the house with me."

"I've heard about the fighting that goes on in the north when chieftaincy is called into issue. Not pretty."

He held her gaze. "My father came by the stool peacefully. No one contested."

She smacked hand over her eyes and groaned. "I've just eaten a meal like a glutton with royalty."

His chuckle warmed the inside of her chest. Would she ever get accustomed to his joviality and how her body responded to it?

"I'd rather one day be called the King of Hiplife."

She hated to disappoint him, but reality had to be faced. "Sorry, but that title belongs to—"

"Me."

"Nope, but how about you being the King of Frenafrohip, considering that you just created a new style of music that's going to be huge."

"Frenafrohip. Frenafrohip." He rolled the word around his mouth as if tasting it. "A combination of French, Afro, and hiplife, right?"

She nodded, impressed that he'd caught on. "It just came to me, but now that I hear you say it, it sounds too heavy. What about Francohip."

"Francohip. I like it even better. How about creating a dance to go with it?"

"You're on your own with that one." Grunting with the stiffness in her joints after sitting for so long, she stood. "Let's finish the last two songs, and then, we'll head home and give you some privacy."

"Or we could relax now and complete them tomorrow. Maybe after you finish church? If you're free."

Before she could answer, Precious yelled from her place on the couch. "We're coming over."

It took her the speed of light to reach the dining room. "I'm sure your poor brains are in need of a rest today. A good sleep will have you refreshed and ready for more work tomorrow."

Lamisi lurched forward when her friend shoved her shoulder.

"Lamisi, Amadu, and I will be here bright and early so you can finish the work." Precious tipped her head to the side and squinted up at Blaise. "Eight in the morning will do nicely."

Who knew her friend could be so easily bought? Give her a gym and a remote control to an enormous plasma screen television, and she took over two people's lives.

Blaise didn't help by smiling. "Eight is fine."

Aunty Vida strolled out of the kitchen. "Wonderful. I'll have breakfast prepared for you, so don't eat before you come."

Precious clapped the cupped palms of her hands together.

"Great." She turned her upper body, but then twisted it back. "By the way, is it okay if we take a dip in your pool tomorrow?"

Lamisi slapped a hand over her mouth with embarrassment while Blaise chuckled. "You have free reign. Enjoy yourselves."

"You're the best, Bizzy. In that case, we have to get going right away. We have some bathing suit shopping to do before the stores close. I'll go get Amadu."

"I'm so sorry," Lamisi muttered. "It looks like your toys are too much for them to resist."

"It's no problem. I hope you're available tomorrow, though."

His voice pitched up with what she took to be concern.

She waved a hand down. "I'm free. Sundays are rest days for most of my family."

"No church?"

The ring of a phone interfered with her answer. She glanced down at the table to see Deola's beautiful, heavily made-up face flashing bright and broad on his screen.

He snatched the phone from the table and swiped it so the ringing stopped.

Air rushed out of her as if she'd been punched in the stomach. He'd claimed that he and the heiress were friends. Then why not answer the call in her presence?

She shook off the sense of betrayal and jealousy. She had no right to either. An ex complaining about her hounding jealousy claimed it had been the reason he'd broken up with her. She'd later discovered that he'd been a lying, cheating, manipulative bastard who had her thinking she might be going crazy when he really had been seeing someone else. She'd been grateful to her ex for inadvertently teaching her the signs of sneakiness in a relationship and that she should always trust her instincts.

Precious and Amadu came trooping up the stairs, discussing the best place to shop for swimming costumes.

Lamisi forced a smile. "We'll see you tomorrow."

They each went to the kitchen to thank and said good bye to Aunty Vida.

The tension between them remained as Blaise walked them out. Her useless chaperones were loading into the car when he leaned down and hugged her close. Her body and mind were not of one accord when she wound her arms around his shoulders and melted into him.

"Thank you, Lamisi. Now I understand why you couldn't stop with expressing the gratitude last week."

He released her before she was ready to leave the nest of his muscular arms.

Tomorrow. She'd committed to helping him, and she would. He owed her nothing, not even the truth about his relationship with Deola. Once she did him this favour, they'd be even, and she wouldn't have to see him again.

CHAPTER SIXTEEN

"Everything had been going well," Blaise complained to Abdul on video chat as he paced the living room an hour after Lamisi and her crew had taken off.

He'd sensed a sudden annoyance in her when Deola's face had come up on his screen. Had she been jealous? He liked the idea of her caring enough about him to be.

His reaction to the call could've been handled better. He'd been taken off guard by how much he'd enjoyed Lamisi's company and hadn't needed Deola's pushy presence disturbing their good time. It had happened anyway.

"Not only is Lamisi magic when it comes to knowing which lyrics need to be translated, but she's cool to hang with. Easy." He kicked the leg of the coffee table hard enough to jiggle the vase of fake flowers. "Deola, on the other hand, only cares about herself and instinctively knows how to ruin things even when she's not around."

Why couldn't he see it before? Even her supposed friendship was toxic.

"What did Deola want?"

He'd returned her call because not doing so would have resulted in a catty, never-ending lecture about phone etiquette. When had he started to allow her have so much control over his life?

"She wanted to convince me that going to the VGMAs together would be better than me going alone or with anyone else because she looked fabulous on camera and knew how to handle the media."

Abdul's frown brought out the brackets at the sides of his mouth. "I told you not to mess with her. Your head got so big when she gave you a little of her attention."

"Whatever, man. I need to get her to back off without hurting her feelings."

"That's a tough one. No one has ever broken off a relationship with her without severe repercussions."

Blaise clenched his fist and tried to keep himself from yelling.

"We aren't dating. We never were. She kissed me once, and it was horrible." He shuddered at the experience. "Wet, sloppy, and I swear that a mouthful of sugar wouldn't have made it any better."

Abdul chuckled. "Sounds disgusting."

"There's absolutely no attraction. No chemistry. Nothing between us."

Unlike with Lamisi. One touch from her, and his skin buzzed. All he'd wanted to do when they were working together was get closer. Nibble on her perfect ears. Slide his lips along her smooth cheek before meeting her mouth, sparking the flames between them.

"Not sure what to tell you. Maybe you should meet with her face to face and let her know how you feel."

"I've already told her. She's a smart woman; she should've gotten it."

Abdul snorted. "Smart and spoiled rotten are two different things. You've heard the stories about what happens when the oil heiress doesn't get what she wants. She had a clothing boutique shut down because they didn't have anything she liked in her size."

Blaise ran a hand over his head and grunted. He'd heard the rumours and even believed that most of them were true. That's what freaked him out.

Someone who had everything going for her shouldn't be so vicious. Damn his ego for getting caught up in wanting to be seen with her.

"You'll figure something out, Blaise. You always do. Now tell me a little more about the new album. Did Lamisi really tear it up with the translation?"

The air became easier to breathe with the change of topic. "Not only that, but she came up with a name for the style."

"Really?"

"Yeah. Check this." He paused. "Francohip."

He could see the wheels in Abdul's head grinding as his friend tipped his face to the ceiling. Blaise knew he'd gotten it when Abdul pumped a fist in the air.

"Aw man, that's hot! A combo of Francophone and Hiplife."

"Exactly."

"She's done well." As if remembering something, Abdul brought his squinting eyes closer to the screen. "Did you sleep with her?"

"No."

Not that he hadn't wanted to since the first moment he'd lain eyes on her. Everything about her appealed to him. He knew without a doubt that she was attracted to him also; yet, she'd stayed away from him instead of calling right away. It would've been for ever if she hadn't needed the favour.

"Blaise." His friend extended the name the way his mother did with a hard hit on the s when trying to draw out the truth from him.

"I haven't."

"Good. Keep it that way. She's not the one for you. She's not Muslim, and your parents wouldn't approve."

The thought of disappointing them was his Achilles heel.

Getting into relationships had never been an issue. Until Lamisi. He hardly knew her, but she made him think of a future as her children's father. His mother had always encouraged that when he found the one, he'd know. Maybe he shouldn't have rolled his eyes at what he now might believe to be sage wisdom.

"Lamisi's mother was a Muslim before she converted to Christianity to marry her father. That should count for something."

Abdul huffed out a sigh. "Unless she's one herself or is willing to convert, then you know as well as I do that it doesn't count. You mentioned you'd be finishing the translations tomorrow."

Blaise murmured his agreement.

"I suggest you cut ties with her after that. Neither of you owe the other anything. The way your eyes glaze over when you mention her name isn't a good sign."

Done with the topic, Blaise asked about Abdul's security firm. His friend delved into the latest development of his new venture, leaving his personal life alone. At least for the time being.

***

Unlike the excitement on the last day of school when she'd been younger, having this be her final time hanging out with Blaise didn't thrill her.

The feeling of unworthiness which had initially kept her away from him had crept back in last night and stuck. He was down to earth and friendly, but he was also a star, accustomed to the glamourous things in life. She was a simple woman who didn't belong in his world. Not like the fashionista Deola.

With good reason, she was sure that women threw themselves at him. She wasn't the sort to share her man. Ever. He'd tire of her and move on—may as well do it before he got the chance.

Why couldn't he be a regular guy living a normal life?

As soon as she parked in front of Blaise's home, he came out.

Amadu stepped up to him first. They shared a handshake ending with a snap. "Hey, man. Thanks for letting us stop by again."

"I owe your sister big time, so enjoy yourself."

"Hi, Blaise." Precious got a short hug while Lamisi hung back.

"How are you doing, Precious?"

"A little sore from my workout yesterday." She held up a bag. "That won't stop me from hitting the gym again. I washed your sister's clothes. Thanks for the loan."

"You're welcome. Breakfast is ready and on the table. Help yourselves."

Precious and Amadu went in without a backwards glance at her.

Unable to resist, despite her newfound resolve, Lamisi initiated the hug. Damn, he felt good. Solid, strong, and right.

"I have a surprise for you after we eat."

Curious, she released him. "What is it?"

His eyes glimmered with mischief. "You'll see."

What could he have planned?

Seeing the buffet spread on the table, all thoughts of his surprise were pushed to the back of her mind as her mouth watered. She filled her bowl with Hausa koko, a smooth porridge made from millet. Skipping over the fried eggs, toasted bread, and oatmeal, she forked koose onto her plate. She held back a moan when she took a bite of the spicy, fried black eyed bean cakes. She had to get the recipe of the best koose she'd ever eaten from Aunty Vida before she left.

The conversation was sparse as everyone focused on the succulent meal. Once plates were empty and multitudes of thanks given to Aunty Vida, they took off to their play spaces.

Lamisi turned to Blaise. "What's my surprise?"

He grinned and stood.

"Follow me." He stopped mid-step. "Bring your driver's license."

She raised a brow. "Why?"

"We don't need issues from the police if they stop us driving the motorcycle."

She clutched her hands to her chest as she looked back and forth between back door and Blaise. Letting out a squeal, she ran in place before crashing into him with a tight hug. "Thank you!"

She hustled to the living room where she'd left her pocketbook, rummaged through her wallet, and pulled out her valid motorcycle driver's license.

"Do you want to see it?"

He chuckled. "No. I trust you."

It must run deep if he was willing to let her drive his motorcycle after the stories Amadu and Precious had told him yesterday. An opportunity should be grasped, not questioned.

With one more leap onto him and a smacking kiss to his cheek, she grabbed his hand and bolted to the side of the house.

Little did he know that he was about to have the most amazing ride of his life.

CHAPTER SEVENTEEN

As they worked on the last song to be translated, Blaise's body still hummed from the residual adrenaline from the motorcycle ride. He'd given Lamisi free reign to go where she wanted. She'd taken to the longest stretch of highway she could find. Being Sunday, the Tema Motorway had been free of the standard traffic found during the week. And then, she'd surprised him by taking the George W. Bush Highway straight to its end in Mallam.

The ride had been as exhilarating as if he'd driven the motorcycle. Her merger of speed and safety as they'd zipped along the road had set him on a natural high. Three hours of driving hadn't seemed to be enough for her when they'd gotten back to his place and removed their helmets.

Her skin glowed, and she couldn't seem to shake her smile. His own had been plastered on his face at having made her so happy.

The translating went smoother than planned. Their minds refreshed, they didn't just complete the last two songs, but went over the ones from yesterday and improved them.

Blaise relaxed with his hands propped behind his head and legs crossed at the ankles.

"We work well together."

"Yes. Well, I'm a language genius."

He nodded. "And you have the flow. I told you."

She hopped up, raised her arms above her head, and flexed her back with a groan.

He rotated to the left as the desire to nuzzle her exposed abdomen threatened to take over good sense.

The chair squeaked as she flopped into it. "It just hit me that I haven't heard you sing the complete songs with the French. We've been doing it all piecemeal."

His moment of embarrassment had come. "I told you that I'm not the best at pronouncing the words."

"Not a problem. We'll go through it line by line."

The faith she had that he wouldn't butcher the language bolstered him.

He pulled up the last song they'd worked on since it was fresh in his mind. For this piece, they'd decided that the chorus would be in French and would start the song. In English, the lyrics were gorgeous, and he did say so himself. He'd been thinking about the woman he'd one day fall in love with as he'd written it.

He looked into Lamisi's dark eyes. Had he unknowingly written the song for her?

Don't be ridiculous. He barely knew her. Although he liked everything he'd discovered so far. Mostly. Her stubbornness could be irritating, but then again, who liked everything about anyone? It would be unnatural.

Just like in his lyrics, her smile made his insides go wobbly.

Hanging out with her felt … right.

Your love sets me free, allowing me to grow
The light in your eyes brings me to my knees
I will love you forever because
with you is where I'm meant to be
I will love you forever because
with you is where I'm meant to be

Lamisi sang it in French to the tune he'd created. He repeated the stanza.

Even to his own ears, the words came out stilted.

The way she bit her bottom lip and grimaced as she listened sent a trickle of sweat gliding down his back.

"That was a nice try," she said with the hesitancy of a teacher to a pupil who'd messed up the answer. "How about if I sing it once and you repeat it?"

She didn't wait for a response. Her sweet, melodious voice did justice to the song, and he got lost in it.

"Now you."

A repeat performance brought on that same disappointed expression.

"Okay." She stretched out the word. "You really need to work on your French. It's a soft language, and you're using it more like a battering ram than a feather."

Ouch. Didn't he like her honest nature? Maybe not at this moment, but he'd learn from her harsh teaching style.

"Let's take the first line and work from there."

Fifteen minutes later, her hair was standing straight out from how often she'd run her hands through it.

She sprang to her feet. "Your lyrics have been translated. I think I've done all I can for you."

"What's wrong? I don't understand."

"Do you want my honest opinion?"

Would his ego survive more of her blatant candidness? "Always."

"Your French is awful. Have you ever heard anyone sing one of your songs and they mess up the language completely, but they joyfully think they've gotten it right?"

He chuckled at her analogy even though he knew where she was going with it. "Many times. Especially when they don't understand the language that it's being sung in."

She rotated her wrist once before presenting her hand palm up with fingers pointing at him. "That's you when you sing in French."

"Come on, I can't be that bad."

"Record yourself and see."

Blaise accepted the challenge. When he played the verse back, he cringed. Horrible. If this had happened in any of the Ghanaian languages or even English, his career would've never gotten off the ground.

He rested his head against the back of the chair and scraped a hand down his face until it rested over his mouth. "What am I going to do?"

His transition into French shouldn't be this difficult. He was a man of rhythm and languages. He'd finally found something that he truly stank at.

The hand she placed on his shoulder brought a comforting warmth.

"From what I can tell, you have three options."

He waited for her to share.

She settled into her seat. "First of all, you could scrap the idea altogether. The songs would sound fabulous in English and the languages you're loquacious in."

Just as he was about to speak, she placed a finger against his lips. He willed himself not to suck it into his mouth and let his tongue sweep over it.

As if realizing what she'd done, she removed her touch and clasped her hands together on her lap.

"I'm spouting ideas. It doesn't mean you have to take any of them."

"Fine. I'm listening."

"The second option is to collaborate with a Francophone singer."

Not bad. It had occurred to him to do it with a couple of the songs, anyway. He'd feel like a fraud if he let someone else sing all of them. It wasn't as if he was starting a boy band or anything. He was a solo artist and would continue to thrive as one.

"The last is that you practice until you speak French like it's your first language. Or at least sing the lyrics as such."

After what he'd just heard come out of his mouth, he wasn't sure about that option, either. "Do you think it's possible?"

She shrugged. "It depends on how much work you're willing to put in."

"Will you help me?"

She snapped her neck so far back that her chin became double. "Um. I'm busy with my dissertation, remember? Busy, busy, busy PhD woman here. No free time."

"Please. I'm willing to put in the work. I really am. I just need a little of your time. Not all of it. Just some."

The fact that it would keep him seeing her was secondary, yet worked out well. He didn't doubt that the more she got to know him, she'd find him irresistible. Just as he found her.

Her twists shook with her vehement rejection. "You should be taught by someone from a Francophone country or get immersed in the language or something like that. That's how I learned how to speak it. I studied French in senior high school and had a couple of classmates from Togo and Côte d'Ivoire who I used to harass into speaking with me. I even followed one of my friends home to Côte d'Ivoire during one of our long vacations. Such an amazing experience."

He'd thought about taking a trip to Côte d'Ivoire, but the idea of going to a non-English speaking country by himself didn't appeal. He grabbed her hand as an idea caught hold.

"I know you're working on your dissertation, but I desperately need your help. Will you travel to Côte d'Ivoire with me?"

With her eyes wide and mouth gaping, he didn't anticipate a favourable response.

CHAPTER EIGHTEEN

Lamisi's parents had taught her to say what she meant because the truth would serve her. She'd learned over the years to soften her words with kindness.

The latter left her current sphere of existence only to be replaced by pure exasperation.

"Are you right in the head? Why would you ask me for such a huge favour when I just told you how busy I am? Why don't you ask Deola to go with you instead?"

She clamped her lips closed at what her temper had let escape. What had gotten into her? A jealousy she shouldn't be experiencing over a man she hardly knew.

It didn't matter. Rather than deal with the issue she'd created, she picked up her things to take her mortified self home. She'd accomplished her mission. It wasn't her fault he couldn't speak French in a manner anyone would understand.

He clasped a hand to the back of his neck and growled.

The action made her dash towards the door.

"Lamisi, please wait."

She stopped and turned at the pleading in his voice. What was she doing running away like a bunny facing a hunter? She was stronger than that.

"As I told you before, Deola is just a friend."

"Okay."

"I should've taken the call when it came through yesterday, but we'd had such a great day, and I didn't want to ruin it."

She crossed her arms over her chest to emphasize her response. "Okay."

He sighed. "The truth is that she likes me, but I only see her as a friend."

"I knew there was something going on between you two. The media doesn't always lie. Everything is based on at least a kernel of truth."

"Except when it comes to anything going on between her and me." He took a step closer. "The attraction is purely one-sided. It's just that she's spoiled and likes to get her way."

Lamisi snorted. "Not surprising for a billionaire oil heiress. She probably gets everything she wants just by raising a finger. What makes you think she won't have you?"

"Because I don't want her." He closed the distance between them by another step. "I never have. I hate to admit this, but I initially saw her as an ego and possible career booster. I was wrong. But then, we got to know each and became friends. Nothing more. It turns out that I really like someone else."

Her heart threatened to hurdle into her throat with its fierce beating. The smouldering gaze he captured her with gave her the answer, but she had to ask anyway. "Who?"

His lips rose in a smirk that made her stomach dip as another agile step brought him even closer. "A woman I recently met. I used to call her mountain woman. After experiencing how she handles a motorcycle, she's now thrill-seeker."

"Oh?"

She'd never had someone be so genuine and forward at the same time. Was she crazy to believe him, or had the charm he'd embroiled her in stolen all of her good sense?

"It turns out that she's my number one fan, even though I would've never guessed it by the way she ignored me the first time we saw each other from across the room."

That brought on an unstoppable grin. "Maybe she'd heard that stroking a musician's ego never turned out well. Better to keep celebrities grounded."

"Yeah, well, I haven't been able to stop thinking about her, and when she called me, I was so excited that I nearly forgot my own name."

Her breath stuttered when he reached out and caressed her cheek with his fingertips. She really should back away.

"Things got even better when this amazing, smart, beautiful woman agreed to help me create a new brand of music. It took a lot of willpower on my part not to touch her while she sat within reach."

Eyes heavy as desire flared, Lamisi stared at his mouth, watching his lips cease their speech as he lowered his head.

The first touch was electric as his lips glided over hers. Her lids closed as she savoured the softness of their firmness. The simple touch turned her inside out with its magnificence. Their lips nibbled and teased in exquisite sweetness.

She'd wanted this moment since the first time she'd lain sprawled on top of him on the mountain.

Blaise's hands spread across her back, pulling her closer to the hard planes of his body. She moaned as she gripped his muscular arms to keep herself upright.

His tongue brushed against her lower lip, and she opened for him. What she'd considered extraordinary just moments ago became earth-shattering as his tongue slid against hers. She circled him, taking in his taste mixed with the fragrance of leather and citrus. A heady, enticing scent.

The earth could implode, and she wouldn't care as long as he never stopped.

Wrapping her arms around his shoulders brought her flush against him.

She whimpered in protest when he slid his mouth to her cheek. The kisses down her jawline brought him to her neck. She stroked the back of his head as he nipped and sucked flesh she'd never known to be sensitive until that moment.

Sliding her hands to cup his cheeks, she raised his head until their lips met again. Passion ran rampant as their tongues swept each other's mouths as if the secrets of life were hidden within.

Her body grew increasingly fevered with the need for more.

When Blaise slid his large palms up her ribcage and touched the undersides of her breasts, she moaned with encouragement. She didn't think to question. Only feel.

His thumbs honed in on her nipples and flicked them, sending a hot flash of desire straight to her core. She lifted her leg to wrap around his thigh. His hardness meeting her centre ripped a groan from her throat.

She hadn't been a virgin for many years, but she'd only just met him in person. It wasn't her style to move so fast with a man. Months, maybe a year, would pass before deciding to make love to a man she'd dated exclusively. Sometimes not at all.

Her logical mind had shut down, replaced with instinct and raw passion. Her body found antiquated societal rules obsolete as she rolled her hips against him. Her hands roamed over the broad expanse of his strong back, gripping his shirt to give her leverage.

"Hey you guy—Oh my goodness!"

Precious's sudden appearance brought reality back to the storm of pleasure.

With only one foot planted on the floor, Lamisi lost her balance when disentangling herself from Blaise. If he hadn't still been holding her, she would've fallen. Another save for him.

When he released her, she smoothed her hands over her top to hide her exposed midriff and help control the jitters.

Mortified that she'd been caught kissing a virtual stranger, she avoided Precious' gaze.

Precious wouldn't let her get away with it. "Lamisi?"

The smirk she witnessed when she looked up matched the amusement in Precious' voice.

She'd get her friend back one day, and revenge would be sweet.

She cleared her throat. "Yes?"

"I'm *really* sorry to disturb. You have no idea how much, but Aunty Vida sent me down to drag you two up for lunch." The grin never left. "She said she'd be leaving early and wanted to make sure you both ate."

Precious pointed towards the entrance. "I could tell her that you're, well, busy."

Lamisi would pay Precious' hair dresser to wash her friend's hair with bleach. That would be a good enough payback for the onslaught of humiliation she kept piling on.

"Please let her know that we'll be there in a minute."

Blaise's voice sounded normal. Unaffected by the torrent of heat still raging through her body.

Rather than leave, Precious stood in the same spot, smiling as if she'd been handed a million Ghana cedis just for being there.

"Precious," Lamisi hissed with a head tick to the side.

"Oh. I'll see you two upstairs."

The finger guns with the corresponding clicks enflamed Lamisi's face even further.

Horrified at her behaviour, there was only one thing she could do. Spine straight, she turned to face Blaise. All shame washed away as she looked into his heated, hooded eyes. She swallowed the apology that had sat on the tip of her tongue.

She wasn't sorry it had happened. His lips called out to her, and angels help her, she wanted to answer.

She took a step back to keep herself from catapulting herself at him. Or was it to give her a better running start?

"We'd better get up there." She winced at her nervous giggle. "We wouldn't want to take up Aunty Vida's free time."

Two steps, and he was within reach. "To be honest, all I want to do is kiss you again."

The flutters in her stomach couldn't be mistaken for hunger. She dropped her gaze to his chest. The same one which had been pressed so firmly against her breasts.

"There's no point."

No longer because of her dissertation. The kiss had disqualified him from including him in the paper. It would be impossible to listen to his voice on the recording of their interview and not remember this encounter. Her work would be filled with bias.

He hooked a finger under her chin and raised it so they were once again eye to eye. No hiding from him.

"Why not? I like you. And I know you like me." One corner of his mouth rose. "You're bad at hiding it. I can see it in your expressive eyes."

Once again caught up in a haze of need, she fought it and removed herself from temptation.

"Deola aside." No, she wouldn't let that issue go. "We're too different."

He cocked his head as his gaze remained steady. "How can you tell? We've only had a couple of days to get to know each other, and most of that time was spent working. I want the chance to acquaint ourselves. Obviously, our bodies know what they want."

Even then, her core throbbed with the desire to be with him. Why was she fighting it so hard? What was she afraid of? Would it be so bad to learn more about him?

"How about if we take things slow?" he offered.

A corner of her mouth tucked between her teeth, she narrowed her eyes to study him. "What do you mean?"

"We go on dates. Chat on the phone. See how things go between us. Just as long as you don't close me out." He sighed as if the truth weighed on him. "I like talking with you, Lamisi. You're interesting and real. When you laugh, it makes my heart do somersaults, and all I want to do is make it happen again. And again. I like seeing you happy, and I'd appreciate the chance to understand you better. And to have you do the same with me."

The man had a way with words, but then after falling in love with his lyrics, she already knew that.

"Can you guarantee that you'll keep me out of the media?"

He shook his head in outright refusal. "Are you kidding? After catching this small glimpse of who you are, all I want to do is show you off to the world. You're amazing. We can keep our personal lives as private as possible, but I can't hide you. It would be like concealing a masterpiece of artwork when all it longs for is to be appreciated. Impossible."

She got lightheaded with the pleasure his declaration induced. Who could say no? Certainly not her. "I can accept slow."

He lifted her. Feet dangling, arms clutching him while she giggled, he swung her around.

"Slow it is."

CHAPTER NINETEEN

For the solid, down to earth man Blaise considered himself to be, he'd somehow transitioned into light and airy since Lamisi had agreed to date him. Even gravity had released its hold to allow him to float. At least in his mind. Magnificent sensations bemused him, eliciting fresh songs that he took the time to jot down when they came to him.

What had happened in the studio with Lamisi before lunch had blown him away. Their honest conversation had changed everything between them. They'd been on fire. From her skittishness, he got the sense that ketchup from a freshly opened bottle would get to its destination long before their relationship got beyond the friendship level.

What was she afraid of? Had someone hurt her?

He'd discover and eradicate her uncertainty. At least, she hadn't shied away from the chance to get to know him.

If only he could use his power of persuasion to influence her in speaking French with him. "Your garden is peaceful and lush."

He snapped out of his thoughts as Lamisi's sweet voice brought him back to the outdoor sanctuary she'd lead him to after lunch.

"Thanks. Being out here gets my creative juices flowing."

She plucked a leaf from a plant next to her when they settled on the wooden bench. "Let's hope it has an impact on your French. Since I'm stuck with you after Precious and Amadu's temper tantrum when I told them we'd leave, we'll try again."

The glimmer in her eyes and the slight upward lift of her lips softened her words.

Did going slow mean he couldn't lean in and kiss her cheek at random moments when he found her adorable? Only one way to find out, so he brushed his lips along her soft skin.

She smiled and touched her fingertips to her face. "What was that for?"

"Because you're beautiful."

A snort wasn't what he'd expected.

"You're going to have to tone it down with the flattery. I know who I am."

Her denial hit harder than a punch to his solar plexus, knocking the wind out of him. He lifted her hand and placed it over his chest.

"I'm not one to flatter anyone, Lamisi. What I mean, I say. Who you think you are and who I see you as seem to be two different people. Your eyes draw me in the same way looking at the ocean does, deep and unfathomable, yet gorgeous to behold. Your nose—"

She waved her free hand in front of his face and sniffled. "That's enough. I don't want to cry in front of you again."

He rested his forehead against hers. "These are tears of ..."

"Overwhelm and happiness that you think I'm beautiful when there are gorgeous women who—"

He cancelled the rest of her words with a quick kiss to the lips. He pulled back so she could see the sincerity he presented.

"Don't compare yourself to anyone else. You are gorgeous, intelligent, witty, strong, and all other sorts of things that I can't wait to find out about. I'm not trying to drive you away, but I know for a fact that you can get someone better than me. I just happened to find you first."

"I doubt that. You're pretty impressive."

He rolled his eyes. "Now who's being charming?"

She giggled and shocked him by tapping her finger on the tip of his nose.

"Do you want to practice your French or not?"

"Not." He laughed. "Let's do it."

"Okay. This time, we'll start saying the words instead of singing them."

As ready as a star pupil wanting to please his teacher, he nodded and waited for her to present the words.

"*S'il te plaît, ne me casse pas les oreilles.*"

"What did you say? I understood please." He pulled at her earlobe. "And ears."

"I said, please don't make my ears bleed."

He laughed. "So that's how it is? I see."

"*Oui.*"

She repeated the sentence.

He mimicked her words.

"Again," she ordered.

Her mouth broadened into a smile after the tenth round of say and repeat.

"That last time sounded just like yours."

She waved her hands like a football match referee calling for the stop of play. "Not at all. It was terrible, but I now understand your problem. You're trying to speak like we do Hausa or even Twi."

"I don't understand."

"French is a soft language. If you don't produce the r's in the back of your throat as if you're rolling it, it will sound flat. And you need to keep your mouth small when you say the vowels."

"I still don't get it."

In her enthusiasm to get her point across, she grabbed his arm. The tingles from her touch distracted him.

"Ewe! To my ear, French sounds more like the language of the Volta Region than any of our other language in Ghana. At least the ones I've heard." Narrowed eyes focused on him. "I've only heard you sing in Ewe once. Do you speak it?"

"As if I was born in Kpando. That's what I spoke with the tour guide on Mt. Afadjato."

She grunted. "I must've missed it when I was trying not to die."

"You made it. At least, you can claim that as your badge of honour."

The removal of her hands left his skin cool. He preferred her warmth, so he entwined their fingers.

Her hand stayed in place. A good sign.

"Say something in Ewe."

He obliged.

"You are a lovely woman who I could stare at all day." He stroked the back of his fingers down her cheek. "Your skin is as soft as the petals of an orchid."

Unable to stop the draw pulsing between them, he brushed his lips against hers and let his breath fan them as he continued in Ewe. "And your mouth causes me to lose concentration and focus on the pleasure of tasting you."

She squirmed out of his arms after her telling shiver and placed both hands against the sides of her face.

"Yeah. Well ... Um." She shuddered out a long breath. "Your Ewe is perfect. And ..." She shifted her eyes to the side and then returned them back to his. "Thank you for the compliments."

***

Amadu's blessed presence in the car on the way home prevented Precious from talking about what she'd witnessed in the studio. Her grin hadn't faded for the whole ride. Amadu had inquired about the lunatic expression, but neither of them had explained.

"Tomorrow. Meet me at *The Cake Boutique* at four," were Precious' parting words when getting out of the car. No option to decline.

The next day, Lamisi adjusted herself on the turquoise seat cushions before taking a sip of the cookie dough and brownie milkshake. None of it made it to her mouth as she drew in her cheeks to suck harder. Giving up, she went into the shop and requested a spoon for the viscous drink.

In the minute it took her to get back to their table, Precious had finished her caramel cupcake.

"Mmm hmm," Precious hummed as she chewed.

Lamisi's eyes drifted closed as the sweet spoonful of milkshake hit her tongue. Precious had made the right call to meet there. It'd been a long time since they'd gotten hyped up on sugar together.

Her phone rang. An unknown number flashed on her screen even through the TrueCaller identifier. Since it could be her supervisor, she picked the call. "Hello."

"Lamisi Imoro?" the feminine voice asked in a harsh tone.

When would people learn basic phone etiquette? "Who is this?"

"Don't worry about it. Are you Lamisi Imoro? Never mind. I know you are. My sources are never wrong."

Sources? She sat up straighter. Could this be related to the heavy breathing calls she'd been receiving? Refusing to confirm the caller's suspicions, she repeated in a sterner voice, "Who is this?"

"All you need to know is that if you keep seeing my man, I'll make your life miserable."

What the hell?

"I have no idea who you are or what you're talking about?"

Precious raised her brows.

"Don't play dumb. You know exactly who I'm talking about. I'm tired of your nasty home-wrecking behaviour. I won't have it. Leave him alone, or completing your dissertation on time, if at all, will be the least of your worries."

Before she could respond to the threat, the line went dead.

Not one to tolerate nonsense, Lamisi called the person back. Beeping sounded before an operator informed her of the number being out of service. She tried once more and got the same response.

She glared at her phone wondering what had just happened.

Her heart beat loud and fast in her ears. Hands trembling, she placed the phone on the table. "That was odd."

"What's going on?"

She relayed the conversation word for word. "I have no idea who she was talking about."

"Could her man be Blaise?"

Lamisi discounted him after the discussion they'd had. She'd believed him when he said he wasn't seeing anyone. "She called me a home-wrecker. I figure the guy is married. Besides, we only just met up again, so no one would ever connect us. Her mention of my dissertation makes me wonder if it's about a guy I assisted with a postgrad course last semester."

"Could be," Precious said with a single shoulder shrug. "Or the woman's man is cheating on her with someone else and she thinks it's you." She leaned in. "Is it you?"

"No," Lamisi growled out.

Her friend laughed. "I didn't think so. You're too much of a stickler for the rules to get involved with your students."

"You're right about that. Plus I had negative zero interest in any of them."

"Doesn't mean they didn't have any in you. And what about your co-workers?"

Lamisi ate her milkshake as she pondered the phone conversation. Could it be a colleague? She rarely engaged with anyone outside of discussing work. Minding her own business was her main priority.

Precious ignored the strawberry cupcake on her plate. "Tell me about what happened with Blaise."

The hairs on her arms rose with exhilaration at the mention of his name. "We kissed."

"I saw that part. Good thing the air conditioner was on because you two would've driven us out with the heat you were generating."

Lamisi shook her head. "It wasn't that dramatic."

"Huh. Your leg was curled around him, Lamisi. And don't think I didn't see where his hands had landed." Precious giggled. "Who knows what piece of furniture might have gotten broken with your activities if I hadn't come in when I did."

She scooped a spoonful of the chilled dessert into her mouth to help cool her embarrassment.

"You know I'm not judging you. In my opinion, you're way overdue for romance. And from what I've learned about Blaise, he's a good guy." She rested her elbows on the table. "What shocked me was that it happened so quickly. One minute, I was harassing you to call him and you're sticking to your guns. The next, you're slathered on him like Nutella on bread."

Lamisi confessed everything that had gone down in the recording studio, including the suggestion to travel with him to Côte d'Ivoire and how she'd been willing to accept his offer of taking things slowly.

"Slow?" Precious screeched. "You two?" She swiped her hands through the air. "No. Never. Not at all. What made you agree to that? Even the hug you guys shared when we left his place sparked up the room. I had to hold Amadu back from flinging you two apart."

Lamisi's leg jiggled under the table as she breathed out through palms cupped over her nose and mouth. Admission time. "He scares me."

Precious tipped her head to the side. "How?"

"He seems too perfect, you know? Plus he's a star who's accustomed to dating stunning, glamorous women. Not someone simple like me." She stirred the spoon in the milkshake, remembering how uncomfortable she'd become when he'd told her about how he saw her. She longed to exemplify the woman he'd described. "Even though I believe him about Deola, I still get a sense that there's more to the story than he's telling me."

"First of all, don't downplay yourself. You're a beautiful, intelligent woman. And you have excellent taste in friends. That says a whole lot about how fabulous you are."

Lamisi chuckled. No one could ever knock down Precious's self-esteem. Her name ensured it.

"You're like a superhero with all the languages you speak and understand. It's not a gift anyone else I've ever met possesses. And you're helping him by using it. Didn't you say that his French is a little better because of how you compared it to Ewe? Who else would've been able to do that? Your skills are saving his musical behind."

Lamisi knew better, but kept her mouth shut. The man was determined, and he would've gotten the work done. It just happened that she'd been around to help him.

She chewed on a chunk of brownie from the milkshake.

"You forget that I've known you forever. He's not like any of your exes." Precious held up a hand when Lamisi opened her mouth to speak. "Those guys who cheated on you were useless scum. They didn't deserve you, and I could see it from miles away. You know me, though. Live and let live."

Lamisi cranked up a brow. "Is that what you were doing when you told me to dump the military man?"

Precious held a palm to her chest. "In my defence, that was the first and only guy I mentioned was bad for you."

Her friend's memory must be slipping with age. "What about the teacher? You butt your nose into every relationship I have. Live and let live, my ass."

"That's neither here nor there. You have to admit that I was right."

The reluctant grunt sounded as her answer. Her friend knew her too well.

"Lamisi, you can't stop dating because you think a man *might* cheat on you. You've declined every guy who's asked you out in the past year."

The go-to excuse came to her lips. "I've been busy with my doctorate."

"You realize who you're talking to, right? That won't fly with me."

She was glad she had someone to hold her accountable.

Precious peeled the paper from her remaining cupcake and took a bite.

"So good," she mumbled around the confection. "Can I make a suggestion?"

As if anything Lamisi said would stop the outspoken woman. "Go ahead."

"You getting your PhD is like me receiving one, too. That's how invested I am in your success. You're too efficient for even me sometimes. I know your schedule of progress. Take him up on his offer to go to Côte d'Ivoire. You'll have a rested brain to tackle the last leg of your research. Spending time alone with him will be good for both of you."

Lamisi blinked several times. "What?"

"I'm not saying you should sleep with him." Precious winked. "Not saying you shouldn't, either."

"Oh my goodness!"

"I want you to loosen up and have a good time. Get to know him on a level you wouldn't while on home turf. I'm sure he's not as well-known there, so you'll be able to roam without worrying about him getting recognized like he would here."

She had a point.

"You'll get to visit Melanie and her family in Abidjan like you've been promising to do for years."

A smile crept onto her face at the mention of their mutual friend.

"And you can stay in the hotel of your choosing. I'd go for one with five stars myself. Take in a couple of concerts so he can get a better ear for the music. You need the break. The tail end of this dissertation has been stressing you out, which has been stressing me. We both need you to go away on vacation and relax.”

They broke out laughing.

“He’s a good guy, and you can glam up like the best of them when you want to. Give him a chance.”

“Are you done with the lecture, Professor Romance?”

She held up a finger. “Just one more thing.”

After several seconds of silence, Lamisi gave in and asked, “What is it?”

“Listen to your instincts. If you had done that when you first met him, you two would probably be married and pregnant with triplets by now.”

Lamisi sucked her teeth at her friend’s silliness. Her point was valid, though. Listening to her gut had never steered her wrong. Where her instincts had wanted to get to know him better, fear of sustaining heartache by the man every woman wanted had made her stay away.

From here on in, she’d trust her heart and see what happened. She’d still be cautious, but at least, she’d give him a chance. Hopefully, he wouldn’t disappoint her.

CHAPTER TWENTY

The flight landed in Côte d'Ivoire the Thursday after Lamisi had surprised Blaise with the offer of escorting him. She'd reminded him that the cost of the venture would be on him. Yet, she'd taken things in hand by organizing the flight and the hotel.

He'd appreciated her consulting with him before confirming any bookings. As if they were a team in making the decisions.

"I'm only here for the weekend," she'd told him. "That's enough for you to get accustomed to the place so you'll be comfortable staying longer if you want to. I think the baptism by fire will allow you to acquire an accent that won't cause your French listeners to curse you out for defiling their language."

He'd laughed at her joke while understanding its seriousness. His career depended on this excursion. At least Armand, his French tutor, had told him he'd been impressed by his improved intonation during their sessions.

In the taxi, on the way to their hotel, Blaise took in the city. He hadn't expected it to be so advanced. After the country's civil wars, he was glad to see that the political strife they'd experienced hadn't damaged too much of the infrastructure, at least in Abidjan.

War could never rival the benefits of peace.

He pulled out his phone and recorded the words. He'd flesh out the song later. In the meantime, he listened to the conversation between Lamisi and the driver like she'd suggested. Understanding everything was impossible, but he wasn't completely lost, either. When he joined in, the driver smiled while Lamisi leaned close and gently corrected him with a whisper.

Tingles coursed from the top of his head down his spine every time it happened. He resisted the temptation of drawing her to his side and seducing her with words that would have her dropping her guard and initiating kisses.

He'd honour their agreement of taking things slow. It was probably better. His parents wouldn't approve of her being a Christian. This had become blaringly clear when he'd presented such a prospect to his mother the other day. She hadn't been happy.

Maybe it would be better if he backed off. An impossible concept to sell to his racing heart when he looked at her. He'd just have to see how things went. Lamisi didn't seem disturbed by him being a Muslim. Maybe she'd be willing to convert before they got married.

Whoa. They hadn't known each other for a month, and he was thinking of marriage? Way too soon.

He shook his head and returned his attention to the view outside the window. This street in Abidjan reminded him of Accra with the hawkers walking amongst the vehicles and selling their wares as they sat in traffic. He looked forward to playing the role of a proper tourist.

The hotel Lamisi had chosen sat in the heart of the city.

The stylish lobby of the multi-story building impressed him—the kind of place that charged in US dollars instead of the local currency of franc.

Having been in his home and learning how much he enjoyed the comforts of life, she'd decided that only the best would do. Yet another positive quality about her. They kept adding up.

After getting settled into their rooms, they met in the hallway thirty minutes later.

"Where are we off to?" he asked as the elevator carried them to the lobby.

"To visit my friend and her family. I haven't seen her in ages. And it will give you a chance to listen and practice in a comfortable setting."

He could handle that. An intimate group to practice with would be better than speaking in front of strangers.

They got into a taxi waiting at the front of the hotel. Lamisi gave the address. The driver programmed it into his phone and then took off.

She turned to Blaise with the biggest smile on her face. "Repeat after me. *J'adore parler français. C'est une langue tellement expressive.*"

He did it … only to have the driver glance at him in the rear-view mirror and chuckle. He knew it wasn't the statement he'd repeated about him liking to speak French because it was such an expressive language.

The driver hadn't blinked when Lamisi had said it.

She slipped her hand into his and squeezed. "Don't mind him. You really are getting better," she proclaimed.

He squeezed back, letting the ego that had gotten kicked in the teeth recover as he relaxed in her reassurance.

***

After years of promising to visit her friend, Lamisi had finally ended up on her doorstep in Côte d'Ivoire. All because of Blaise.

The conversation with Precious had freed up whatever had bound her. She'd determined herself as worthy of everything and everyone she desired, including the soon-to-be King of Francohip. Not all men were the same. She needed to keep that on a loop in her mind, and everything would work out.

Melanie's screams when she opened the door brought out Lamisi's own squeals as they hugged.

The French flowed fast and furious as the world dropped away.

"It's so good to see you again. Why did it take you so long to get here?" Melanie asked as she held both of Lamisi's hands and cut off the circulation to her fingers.

"I could ask the same." Lamisi pushed her bottom lip out into a deep pout. "When was the last time you stepped foot in Ghana to visit me?"

"Oh, no, my friend, you will not turn the tables. All blame goes to you."

Lamisi giggled.

"It's so good to see you. You look magnificent." Her gaze fell to Melanie's pregnant belly and then up to her rich dark brown skin. "You're glowing."

Melanie turned in a circle.

"Thank you. My baby is fantastic. I feel good most of the time, and I only have two more months to go." She rubbed her abdomen. "I can't wait to meet her."

"Me, too."

A clearing of the throat brought the women's attention to the entrance.

Two pair of eyes stared at the chocolate-skinned, tall, athletic, heart-wrenchingly handsome man flashing his gleaming teeth at them.

Lamisi took the couple of steps to reach him and rested a hand on his arm.

"Blaise Ayoma, this is my good friend, Melanie Ettien."

The two shook hands.

"It's a pleasure to meet you, Melanie," Blaise said in French.

At least, it no longer made Lamisi's eye twitch.

Melanie smiled when she responded in her colonial language. "You, too."

Her gaze didn't wander from Blaise's face for several seconds as her brows creased together.

An unfamiliar sense of possessiveness drove Lamisi to lean in close enough to him so their arms touched. She ignored him when, from her peripheral vision, she noticed him glance down at her.

Melanie shook her head and blinked.

"Please," she said in English. "Pardon me for staring. It's just that you look familiar." And then, her eyes lit up, and she snapped her fingers with excitement. "Oh, my. You're the Ghanaian hiplife artist Bizzy."

She reached out and took his hand, shaking it so hard that the strong man's body vibrated. "My friends won't believe this."

"How about a picture for proof?"

"Okay." Melanie picked up her phone from the table, tapped the screen a few times, and thrust it at Lamisi.

Amused, Lamisi took the photos. So much for him not being recognized in Côte d'Ivoire. "It seems your reach is farther than you thought."

"I'm glad to hear it," he said.

Melanie touched the hair she'd bunched into a loose bun and looked down at herself. Then she turned hot eyes in Lamisi's direction. *"Oh mon Dieu, Lamisi. Pourquoi ne m'as-tu pas dit que tu amenais quelqu'un? Regarde-moi, je suis dans un piteux état."*

"On the contrary." He said in the sexy voice that held a catch of breath. "You're as far from a mess as can be. You're radiant," he replied in English.

Lamisi laughed at her friend's gaping mouth. "He understands some French. He doesn't speak it as well as he should … yet. That's why we're here. And of course, to visit you."

"Yes." The English had returned. "You are more than welcome. Bizzy, where are my manners? Have a seat."

"Please, call me Blaise."

Melanie nodded with an unrelenting grin. "Blaise."

They settled in the living room of the cute single-story home.

"Excuse me while I bring you some water."

Hospitality, just like in Ghana, reigned with their neighbouring country. No one came into their home without receiving water. The choice was up to the guest whether they'd drink it or not, but it was always presented.

"Melanie is a bit vain. I'm shocked she agreed to the picture. In her excitement, she must've forgotten that she wasn't dressed to the nines," Lamisi gossiped. "I'm sure she'll return in a floor-length sparkly evening gown and a fully made-up face."

Blaise laughed. "I can't believe she recognized me."

"Me, neither. Considering she spent her senior high school years in Ghana, maybe she follows the music."

She shrugged to downplay it, the selfish part of her not wanting him to be famous here. A nice, normal time of getting to know each other would suit her better.

"It would be helpful if I had a fan base here. It'd make breaking into their music scene easier."

She waved down a hand. "Don't worry, with the songs you've created, you'll have no difficulty getting the people of this, and all the other Francophone countries, to love you."

His eyes softened as he slid closer to her. The kiss on her cheek was unexpected. Heat flushed her face.

"What was that for?" One day, she would become accustomed to his random acts of affection rather than questioning it.

He caught her fingers in his. "I appreciate your support. Not once have you told me I couldn't make it. Or told me I should give up."

She hadn't been perfect. "I presented it as an option."

"As part of the truth I needed to acknowledge because you were right about me sucking at French. But then, you helped me."

He kissed the back of her hand.

A spiral of warmth settled in her chest.

"And now, you're spending time you could be using to work on your dissertation to help me even more. I can't express how much I appreciate it."

She wasn't as altruistic as he made her out to be. Should she tell him about the need she had to get to know him? The part about gaining a temporary break from school to relax and refresh her mind? A mini vacation that he was privileged to pay for?

She didn't get the chance. Her mouth was silenced when his lips brushed against hers, reminding her of their first kiss. If she were going to start something with him, she may as well be completely honest, at least physically.

She reached her free palm up and grazed his cheek as he dove back in. His lips, full yet firm, nibbled hers. Demanding, yet yielding. She could kiss him for the rest of the time they had together, but the throbbing at her core told her it would lead to more than she was ready for.

The sound of something banging pulled her out of the magical experience of his touch.

Prying her eyes open, Lamisi held back any sense of awkwardness as Melanie hovered above them holding a tray with a large bottle of water and two glasses beside it.

The woman had changed into a red sequined top that stretched over her extended belly, a black skirt that flirted with her knees, and heels that her doctor would most likely warn her against wearing in her condition. And yes, the makeup was present and in full force.

Holding in her laughter to the point where she thought she'd burst a major blood vessel, Lamisi stood and hugged her friend. It was nice to know that while Blaise was disrupting her world, some things never changed.

CHAPTER TWENTY-ONE

Blaise and Lamisi had spent the taxi ride back to the hotel in silence. He figured she was all talked-out after the hours spent with her friend. He'd intermittently watched French-speaking television shows and listened to their conversation. Most of both had been lost on him.

They hopped out of the taxi at their temporary residence.

"Thanks for taking me to meet Melanie," he said when they met up on the sidewalk. "I feel like I intruded on your time with your friend."

"No worries. We talk all the time on the phone. It was just a matter of seeing her after so long that hit us."

He rubbed his stomach. "She didn't have to feed us so much."

"That would be like telling Aunty Vida not to do the same. Melanie is one of the most gracious people I've ever known. You'll never leave her home without needing to spend the night, or at least take a nap, because you're so stuffed." She winked at him. "I saw you dozing for a few minutes there."

"Guilty. I still need to burn off some of the food. Want to take a walk?"

"Sure."

The sun was starting to sink in the sky, casting a golden pink light to view their surroundings. Abidjan reminded him of the main areas of Accra with the human and vehicular traffic trying to get home after a long day.

Competing with restaurants, vendors sold food at the roadside. Grilled fish and fried plantain scented the air. Instead of the hot kenkey made with corn dough that was an evening staple at home, the residents here preferred attiéké.

He'd been wary of the pellet-like food made from cassava when Melanie had presented it to them after they'd washed their hands. It had been complemented with fried fish and a concoction created from peppers, onions, tomatoes, oil, and spices.

He'd watched how the ladies ate. Just like with many foods in Ghana, no utensils were necessary. He'd liked the mild flavour of the steamed cassava and hadn't refused when Melanie had offered more.

Music came from Lamisi's bag. She dug through it and pulled out her cell phone. Her lips flattened into a tight line as she slammed her finger into the face of the screen, making the ringtone stop.

"Who was that?"

Did he have a right to ask? The fact that the call had irked her dropped a boulder of dread in his stomach.

She flicked a hand. "Someone calling from an unknown number. I've blocked it every single time, but she calls from different lines because it always comes through."

The hairs on the back of his neck stood as the skin of his scalp tightened. Was he just feeling her own irritation? He'd always been sensitive, but never this empathetic. "Maybe they're coming from different people."

"I doubt it. I answered once, and the woman threatened me. I'm pretty sure she was crazy because I had no idea what she was talking about. Ever since then, I don't pick up unknown calls."

His agitation heightened as thoughts of Deola pinged across his brain. It couldn't be her. As an unknown in the entertainment world, Lamisi was off everyone's radar. He tamed the idea of Deola's involvement. It seemed unlikely.

The mystery still needed to be solved.

"What did she accuse you of?"

"It doesn't matter because it isn't true." She crossed her arms over her chest with a definitive nod. "I don't want to talk about it anymore. I'm sure she'll get tired of playing her idiotic games if I don't indulge her. She'll realize the truth of her mistake soon enough."

The protector in him roared inside with the need to take care of her problem. Find a solution that wouldn't leave her stressed each time her phone rang. The independent woman had made up her mind to handle it her way, and he'd respect her decision even if he didn't like it.

The least he could do was offer his assistance. "Let me know if you need me to do anything. I'm always willing to help."

"Thanks."

He budged her shoulder with his. "You're saving my career. I'm in your debt."

"Language is my life. It's my pleasure to assist."

"Thanks for the lesson you had Melanie give me on my French. I think it helped."

She smiled up at him. "With each encounter, you're improving. Soon, you'll sound like a local."

Her encouragement swelled his heart. "I hope so. By the way, I don't mind if you ditch me to spend time with Melanie. I didn't realize that coming here would be so much like Accra. Now I know and can handle it. You don't need to be my guardian."

"You're stuck with me and my tutorials, Bizzy. Melanie and her husband are travelling to visit her parents in Lakota early tomorrow and will return on Sunday. We'll stop by before our flight back to Accra."

"I don't mind." He downplayed his excitement at being able to spend time with her. "What do you have planned for us?"

"I read somewhere that you're Muslim. If you agree, since tomorrow's Friday, I thought we'd attend *ṣalāt al-jum'ah* at the Mosque of Plataea. It's a gorgeous structure."

"Technically, yes, I am, but not practicing," he answered. "Well, other than not eating pork or drinking alcohol. Along with the basic principle of respect ingrained within the religion, I'm not a practitioner."

"Oh." The sides of her mouth drooped. "I didn't know that."

At least, he'd been able to keep one thing away from the public.

His heart raced as a revelation clicked. He stopped walking to look at her in the light transitioning from natural to artificial. Someone behind them almost rammed into him. He was happy to have recognized the insult thrown at him in French.

Blaise pulled Lamisi closer to the building they'd stopped near. "You said we'd attend service there. Is that for my benefit?"

She blinked up at him. "I may not be the most devout Muslim, but I like to attend *jum'ah* every once in a while."

His legs threatened to buckle. The one thing he'd worried about had been a moot point. Better to clarify just in case his stomach using up most of his blood in food digestion had left him delusional.

"Are you a Muslim?"

"Yes."

Amazed, it took him a beat to speak again. "How? Why?"

She shrugged. "It's the religion I identify with most. My parents raised us as Christian, but they encouraged us to explore and find our own spirituality. My mother was a Muslim who chose Christianity when she married my father."

"Why did you pick Islam over Christianity?"

"I didn't. Not really." She spread her arms out wide and formed a circle with them by linking her hands. "It's all the same thing. The same God with different names and too many misunderstandings between the people who practice their faiths to let them comprehend this."

He nodded in complete agreement. "Even within religions, there are differences and disagreements."

"Exactly. It would be better for the world if we realized that we're all one."

She'd spoken the words he'd been trying to live all his life. "True."

"I've practiced as many religions as I could discover. Islam resonated within me." She held a palm towards him as if to halt him from speaking. "I'll be the first to admit that it's not perfect. After all, it's a religion. But I like the way it respects the beliefs of others because Allah is the God of us all."

She lifted a slim shoulder and let it drop. "It's what I've been practicing ever since. Perhaps not as well as I should, but I try. Sometimes—"

Blaise leaned over and kissed her hard on the lips. Even that brief touch stirred a yearning in his chest. He wanted more, but held back.

The country had been colonized by the French, but Africans in general tended to be conservative. Kissing in public, especially the way he longed to delve into the warmth of her mouth, would be frowned upon.

Her tongue flicked out and licked her lips, keeping his attention there. Her gaze flittered to their environment before returning to his eyes. "Why'd you kiss me?"

Because you're extraordinary in every conceivable way and it hurts my muscles to restrain myself from touching you.

"It's a celebration of you being Muslim."

One more reason to appreciate that they might belong together. They'd only know for sure with time, but so far, he could envision being with her long term.

Now to make her see it.

CHAPTER TWENTY-TWO

The colossal mosque held a magnificent glory that Lamisi had never experienced before in a place of worship. Inside and out. Did Blaise being by her side before they'd split into their designated male and female areas have anything to do how her spirit had lifted with excitement?

She stepped out of the women's area of the mosque feeling fulfilled and connected to Allah and his creation. It took a while for her to catch sight of Blaise's wide-shouldered stance, towering height, chocolate skin, and defined features among the exodus of males. Her breathing hitched when he came into view. Stunning.

His dark eyes searched the female portion of the crowd. When his gaze met hers and he smiled, time stood still. Her heart threatened to lurch out of her chest with the force of its beats. She took her time descending on shaky legs to meet him at the bottom of the stairs.

"Hi," she managed to get out in a low, breathy voice, caught up in the fact that this man wanted to be with her.

"Hey. How was the service?"

"I loved it. Almost makes me want to become completely devout." She held up a finger knowing it would never happen. She enjoyed spirituality more than the religious aspect. "Almost."

He chuckled.

"I understand what you mean. The place is spectacular. The energy in the atmosphere transcended me to a state of being ethereal." He held out his hand and it quivered. "Even now, I'm having trouble acclimating to my body."

He'd expressed her sentiment in such an articulate manner. If they weren't at a mosque, she'd be the one to plant a kiss on him. "Me, too."

Ready to leave the space where people continued to flow around them, she stepped to the side and bumped into someone.

Lamisi recognized the man's Arabic roots when she looked at him.

"*As-salāmu'alaykum. Ana asfeh.*" She greeted in Arabic and then apologized.

The man stopped and cocked his head before returning her greeting of peace. "*Wa'aleikum salaam Wa-rahmatullahi wa-barakatuh.*"

He then asked if she spoke Arabic.

"Yes, I do," she responded in his language and watched as his bearded face smiled. Before he could ask her any further questions, she added, "One of my former colleagues in Ghana was Lebanese. When we became friends, I picked up her language."

The handsome man, somewhere in his early thirties, stepped closer. Blaise's heat touched her from behind.

If the man's wide eyes were any indication, he was impressed. "You learned Arabic by ear?"

"Yes. Languages are a gift of mine."

"No matter what else you may speak, Allah has blessed you abundantly with the language of Arabic."

Laughter sprinkled out of her.

"I see." She continued the conversation in his language. "My friend told me something similar."

Blaise cupped a hand over her elbow. A show of possessiveness that elicited a bubbling giddiness in her chest.

She glanced up at him. His narrowed eyes and snarled upper lip were directed at the stranger.

"We should get going," Blaise said in English, his voice deeper than normal.

She recognized jealousy when she saw it. She probably shouldn't be so happy about it, but when had anyone cared about another man's response to her? Never.

"It was nice speaking with you," she said in English to keep Blaise in the conversation.

The man's eyes rose to Blaise's face, and he stepped back with a nod. "*Etsharafna, ma' el salameh.*"

With a contagious grin and a lift of his hand, he left.

Blaise stalked the guy with his eyes. "What did he just say?"

She shrugged to keep the situation light while her insides danced. "That I'm the most intriguing woman he's ever met, and he wished my overbearing bodyguard weren't around to block his chances."

He stepped closer, towering. "He didn't say all of that."

"The language is word efficient." She took off down the street towards the hotel with her hijab still covering her head as the mosque mandated for women to worship. She needed to change out of her long-sleeved top and ankle-length skirt into something more heat-friendly.

He strode down the street with her. "You can stop playing now. What did he say?"

"He told me it was nice talking with me and that I should take care."

"Huh. On the mountain, you told me that you speak eight languages, but what are they? I don't want to be shocked the next time one comes flying out of your mouth."

She chuckled. "Let's see. I'll count Twi and Fante as one because they're both Akan. English, French, Hausa as you very well know, Ewe—which I picked up from Precious, Ga which is my father's tribe, Dagbani, from my mother's people, and Arabic."

No longer afraid to boast for fear of overwhelming him, she smirked. "I understand more languages than I speak, so please don't think you can talk about me in front of my face and get away with it."

His shoulders shook with his booming laugh. "I'm sure that even if I created my own language, you'd be able to understand. You have an uncanny way of reading people, not just understanding what they say."

She stared at him in wide-eyed awe. He'd noticed that about her? What else had he gleaned? Maybe that she was still scared about getting involved with him although she thought she might almost be ready.

Shaking fears from the past proved harder than people who said, "Get over it," made it out to be.

"What if I told you to your face that I find you to be incredible?" he said in Hausa. The language streamed beautifully and resonated within her. "From what I've encountered and seen of you, you're generous with your time and soft-hearted towards those you love. You smile freely at people you don't know, which I'm sure brightens their day as much as it does mine." He tapped the centre of his chest. "It has the ability to make my heart flutter."

She bowed her head, cheeks bunched with her grin. The man was too much. No one other than him had ever spoken to her in such a poetic manner before.

Not the time to act shy. Raising her head, she pulled her shoulders back and looked up into his eyes. "Thank you."

"My pleasure."

They reached the hotel a few minutes later.

"After I change, I thought we'd get something to eat. Melanie recommended a few places in the same area. We could check them out and see which one is the best."

"Cool."

They headed up to their rooms. At their doors, Blaise reached out for her and pulled her into a hug. She wound her arms around him and leaned her head against the strength of his shoulder.

Hadn't she wanted this for the past week? The security of being in a man's arms thrilled her. She willed him to hold her for the rest of the trip. For the rest of her life.

She snapped her eyes open as terror clawed at her. Thoughts of the future with someone she was still getting to know weren't supposed to be in her scope of thought. Maybe heat had gotten trapped in her skull from wearing the hijab. She released him, and he followed suit.

The kiss to her cheek eased her trepidation. Moments like this made her feel as if he cared and could also see them progressing through life together. If she were more confident, she'd capture his lips and kiss him as if he were the last thing her mouth would ever devour.

He pulled away, leaving her body to cool.

"Whenever you're ready," he whispered. "I'm here."

She didn't need to ask what he was referring to. Taking things to another level would require more than a few days of interacting. The prickly warmth of her skin at his offer told her differently.

Listening to her body would make things complicated when she wanted simplicity.

Too late.

CHAPTER TWENTY-THREE

Lamisi flopped across her hotel room bed at the early hour of nine p.m. and let out a huge yawn. The day spent with Blaise had been perfect. Not only did the locals no longer do a double-take and snicker when he spoke their language, but they'd had fun.

Blaise's talent wasn't limited to constructing song lyrics. Jokes also featured on his specialty list.

A day of exploring Abidjan had included a beautiful walk on the beach and a dinner of fresh grilled red snapper paired with her now favourite attiéké. She hadn't wanted the day to end. To be apart from him.

Serious, PhD-oriented Lamisi disappeared when they were together, replaced by the giggly teenager she'd once been. Anyone who knew her would be surprised at how laidback she was when with Blaise.

It must be the fact that he didn't seem to take much seriously. Granted, he was a focused man and knew how to handle issues. Yet, his main priority seemed to enjoy life.

"What's the point of worrying when it won't solve anything? Live in the here and now. The rest will take care of itself when the time comes."

He'd spoken without diverting his gaze from the brilliant clarity of the sea when she had complained about how much more work she still had to do on her dissertation.

A philosophy she could totally get with. And would. Maybe even when he wasn't around.

The sparks kept passing back and forth with each touch, accidental or otherwise. A delicious warmth had found a new home tucked under her ribs when he gazed into her eyes. She'd focused a lot of her attention on his mouth when he spoke, not only wanting to hear his words, but feel them against her lips. Proof that entering his room tonight when he'd invited her to watch a movie and hang out would've been a bad idea. One that might've led to a physical intimacy she wasn't yet ready for.

She'd barely started to trust him—sleeping with him this early was out of the question. At least, that's what her mind kept reiterating. Her body, on the other hand, wanted to climb all over him and finish what they'd started in the studio last week.

A gentle knock on his door wearing a robe with nothing underneath would lead to an invite inside.

Her core throbbed as her fantasy went into overdrive as she slid her robe down her body so it pooled on the floor before she stripped his clothes off.

She hopped out of bed, clearing her mind of him kissing her into oblivion as his hands roamed over her body, driving her to the pinnacle of need that compounded the one she already had for him.

The water would relax her while washing away the sea salt that the refreshing ocean air had deposited on her skin.

Thirty minutes later, she was sure the residents below her would come up and tell her to cut out the pacing. The activity kept her hands from twisting the metal handle that would release her from the room. She strode the few steps it took to get to the wardrobe cabinet where she'd stored her laptop.

A muffled noise came through the wall on Blaise's side. When his voice got louder, curiosity wriggled under her skin. What had happened to make him sound so upset?

Not my business.

Then why was her ear against the cool painted plaster, being incredibly rude by eavesdropping?

"How did you find out about Lamisi?"

The mention of her name was the sole justification for continuing to listen when she knew better.

"Don't try to change a subject that you brought up, Deola. I asked you a direct question."

She covered her mouth to keep from gasping as her heart clanged against her ribcage. She'd never make a good spy. Why was his *friend* talking about her?

"I told you before that I'm not taking you to the VGMAs. In fact, the way you've been behaving lately, I think we should take a break from our friendship."

A low feminine screech reached through the wall.

"I'm not someone in your command. If you can't respect me and my decision not to get involved with you, then we can't continue as friends. Lamisi has nothing to do with you, so you'd be better off forgetting her name. I'm *not* your man. I never have been and never will be. It's time you understand that."

His voice sounded strained, as if attempting not to let everyone in the hotel know his feelings on the matter.

This time, the pause lasted for much longer than the previous ones. Deola must be having her say. Was she the type of woman who'd beg? If she were anything like Lamisi, she'd let Blaise go.

Then again, he was an extra type of special. Would she fight for him?

She didn't know.

When Blaise finally spoke, his voice was too low for her to hear. Lamisi looked around for anything that would amplify sound. Where was a stethoscope when she needed it?

What was that creaking noise? She leaped away from the wall with her hand on her chest when a door slammed shut.

Okay. The conversation hadn't ended to his satisfaction. Had Deola been convincing enough to retain a position in his life?

And then, a red bulb went off in her head. Was Deola the one stalking her through calls and texts? Had the woman been so threatened by her that she'd stooped so low?

Given the situation, Lamisi smiled. She'd never been anyone's object of envy before. Much less a wealthy, world-famous heiress. She thrust her shoulders back with pride and strutted to the side of the room she should've been on the whole time rather than listening to Blaise's conversation.

Now that she was at least eighty-five percent sure of who'd been behind her stress for the past couple of weeks, it no longer held her captive. She could look at the phone, give the petty woman a millisecond of her time, and then carry on as if it had never happened.

Lamisi would wait Deola out. She'd get tired of playing her petty games.

CHAPTER TWENTY-FOUR

Blaise swayed his upper body to the beat while listening to a zouglou song by an Ivoirian artist that he admired. The lyrics held more meaning as he repeated them as Lamisi had instructed.

So far, their weekend had been the best he'd had in a long while. Being with her was like breathing in the fresh, clean air from his hometown.

Easing her into his more affectionate manner put a strain on him when he wanted to shower her with kisses, random caresses, and words that would melt her resistance. He'd kept things light by brushing her hair off her face when the wind blew as they walked hand in hand on the beach yesterday.

The hug they'd shared at the end of the night before separating to their own rooms had stoked a strong desire to stay by her side. To hold her all night while they talked, nothing more.

He refused to let himself recall how responsive her lips had been the week prior. It would've just driven him insane with a need he couldn't fulfil.

Deola's call last night had perturbed him. She'd been tenacious about attending the music award ceremony together as if he'd never told her they wouldn't. He'd been firm in his rejection. Even though her outrage had vibrated through the phone, he hadn't back-tracked.

And then, she'd mentioned Lamisi by her full name in a casual comment which had aimed to manipulate. His head had nearly exploded with rage when she'd refused to reveal her source. She'd either been having him followed, or one of his boys had betrayed him.

Protecting Lamisi had become his main priority. He'd deal with how Deola had discovered her information later. No longer caring about upsetting the heiress, he'd broken off their friendship. Or at least tried to. Her tearful pleading had touched his sensitive side.

He'd given her one more chance. Although the woman lived a privileged life, she had few friends, and when her guard was down, came off as lonely.

He'd ended up putting stipulations on their relationship. She wasn't to mention Lamisi. Had to keep things platonic. And there would be absolutely no manipulation.

Thinking back on the conversation, he should've let her drop. If the rumours were correct, Deola's lack of friendships was due to her controlling, vicious, and vindictive nature. He didn't need the hassle.

He'd stormed out of his room to stretch his legs and exhaust his ire with a walk. When he'd returned long after midnight, he'd raised his knuckles to rap on Lamisi's door, but had stopped himself at the last second. His feet had dragged along the carpeted floor to his room.

Now he stood at her door at a reasonable hour, looking to take her out on another tour.

Lamisi swung the panel open wearing a sleeveless pink, blue, and cream-coloured batik print dress that hugged her waist and flowed out over her hips to her knees. She had applied a light layer of makeup that brought out her cheekbones, dark eyes, and full lips.

He leaned against the wall as she stared, hoping he looked cool instead of a man whose knees had just gone weak.

She touched her fingertips to hair she'd pinned away from her face. "What?"

"You look wonderful."

"Thank you. Are you ready to go? I have a full day planned."

No trying to get him to gush over her. No denying her own beauty. Just a confident answer from a strong woman. He looked forward to the experience of falling more in like with her.

After eating breakfast in the hotel restaurant, they went to the local market and interacted with the market women. His ears picked up a lot from the atmosphere. When he repeated snippets of what he had learned to Lamisi, she beamed up at him.

"You sound good."

The feeling of pride would last until he messed up again.

"It's a process," she reassured with a pat on the arm. "Keep trying. I know you'll get it."

The confidence she had in him made him want to succeed for her almost as much as for himself. Once again, he slid down the slippery slope of admiring her even more.

Following the local market, they went to a shopping mall. The interactions with the people in the modern space weren't as frequent, but he did get some practice in.

During their lunch at the food court, they released the student-teacher role, enjoying the meal and each other as they talked about their family and childhood. Many of the stories they told had them laughing to the point of drawing attention from their neighbours.

After one more round through the massive mall to help settle their food, he tugged her to the glass and metal railing where they watched people going about their business. "How about we return to the beach and relax until it's time to head off to visit with Melanie?"

Lamisi shook her head. "Not on the agenda."

He wished he could add some kissing onto the list of things planned to do. He had trouble focusing on anything but her reapplied gloss over such luscious lips.

"Then what is?"

She tipped her head, exposing the side of her neck. He brushed his lips against the area. From the way she leaned into him, she had also forgotten about the public space they were still in.

Blaise flicked his tongue against her soft skin, eliciting a moan from her. He raised his head to find her eyes closed with her mouth slightly parted. He gripped the railing until his palms hurt and faced the other side of the mall to prevent himself from breaking further social norms and kissing her full on the mouth.

His heart slowed to normal as he focused on people-watching.

Lamisi positioned herself to face him head-on. "As much as I'm appreciating the air-conditioning, we should get going."

"Where to?"

She grinned and wiggled her brows. "You'll see."

He appreciated her teasing, but not her announcement. "I'm not a fan of surprises."

"Okay, then let's call this an examination of sorts."

When she took off towards the end of the mall, he stayed in place, watching her hips sway and making the dress flounce around the back of her cinnamon-hued skin.

She glanced over her shoulder to find him observing her. Halting mid-step, she pivoted and returned. "I promise that you'll like it."

"How do you know?"

"A gut feeling. Besides, it's better that you know this about me now."

Interest had him standing at his full height, making her tilt her chin to look into his eyes. "What?"

"When it comes to languages … and one or two other things, I tend to be right all the time."

He smirked, piqued by curiosity. "Is that so?"

"Come with me and see."

The one invitation was all it took to accept her challenge.

CHAPTER TWENTY-FIVE

Lamisi took him to the last place he'd ever expect to end up while in Abidjan. A barber shop.

He ran a hand over the short bush on his head. "I don't need a cut."

"It's not about the haircut. It's about the interaction." Grasping his shoulders with both hands, she caught his gaze. "Your mission is to go in there and speak only French. No other language will be allowed."

"Why a barber shop when we can do it anywhere? What if they butcher my hair?"

Unable to help herself, she reached up and smoothed her fingers over his head. The dark coils sprang under her touch, and he shivered when she caressed the base of his hairline.

What he'd started in the mall lingered, and her neck tingled with the memory of his kiss. His lips the only thing in sight, she stepped closer to diminish the unnecessary gap between them.

The door to the shop opened, letting out raucous laughter from inside.

Disappointed, she hung her head and dragged in a deep breath. She turned to the glass panel to see that men and a couple of women were looking at them, hooting. Head on fire, she dropped her hands to her sides and stepped to the left, out of their view.

Lamisi risked looking up into Blaise's face and found him grinning. She'd met the most irresistible man in the world. Either she learned how to deal with it, or she'd end up falling into their attraction every time they were together. Privacy be damned.

She cleared her throat. "This is where Melanie's husband has been getting his hair cut for the past fifteen years. As you witnessed from the number of people waiting inside, it's a pretty popular place. I called the owner and told them Bizzy would be stopping by for a cut and chat." She flung up a finger. "In French only. The guy said he was a fan of yours. Do you want to disappoint a fan?"

He chuckled. "Since you put it that way ..."

"Good. Don't worry. I'm sure they'll take it easy on you. When you're done, we'll head over to see Melanie."

He tugged her deeper into the shadow of the building. Her mouth dried at the passion in his eyes just before he lowered his head to her and slid his lips against her mouth. "When do we get to be alone?"

Lifting her heavy lids, she gazed into his eyes, her mind hazy. "Um."

"Hey, Bizzy."

The familiar voice of the barber shop owner asking if he was going in lulled into her head.

Blaise kept his gaze glued to her for a moment longer before pivoting his head to the left. "*Oui, j'arrive.*"

Lamisi regained strength in her legs and followed him into the shop to observe the magic of black men bonding over the buzz of clippers and snipping scissors.

***

Blaise and Lamisi sat side by side in the taxi for the late-night ride back from Melanie's place.

He skimmed a hand over his head. The barber had done as he'd asked and faded him out on the sides. The conversation flying around him at the barbershop had made him laugh so much that he'd forgotten about being self-conscious of his French and had participated when he could. Glimpses of Lamisi grinning as she flipped through a magazine had told him he was doing well.

The guys at the shop had been accommodating and gracious when he'd messed up. They'd stayed for an hour after the owner had removed the cape and dusted off the excess hair because the positive vibes of the place had been conducive to learning.

"Good job today," she said once they'd packed into a taxi to head back to the hotel.

"Thank you. Since it was an exam, what grade will you give me?"

She cocked her head and tapped her chin as if thinking. "An A for effort and being a good sport. And a B minus for your pronunciation."

"I'm impressed with myself. It's better than the F you would've given me last week." He intertwined their fingers. "I couldn't have gotten this far without you, Lamisi. Thank you."

Her grin squeezed his heart.

"Glad I could help."

He heard the residual tension in her voice. She hadn't been herself, at least what he knew of her while they'd visited with Melanie and her husband. Instead of the intense focus she could give to a conversation, she'd seemed side-tracked and a bit jumpy.

"You seemed a little preoccupied with your phone this evening." Blaise broke the comfortable silence. "Is everything okay?"

"Since you asked." With a sigh, she untangled herself from him and pulled her cell from her bag. A couple of screen slides later, she held the device out to him.

"This message slipped through my radar before what I was reading registered."

'I told you to stay away from my man. Since you don't know how to listen, bitch, I'll just have to show you what happens to people who cross me.'

Not believing his eyes, Blaise read the message again before giving her his attention.

Lamisi twisted her hands together. "I've narrowed down my stalker to one person."

Ready to do damage to whoever was causing her such turmoil, he asked, "Who?"

She stared at him in a way that made him question if she thought he was the guilty individual. "Your friend, oil heiress Deola Olajumoke."

He believed her. Deola mentioning Lamisi during their conversation last night gave him no other choice. He rubbed a hand over his face.

"After what I heard you say through the wall last night," she continued, "I don't doubt that it's her."

"What?"

She dropped her gaze. "I didn't mean to eavesdrop, but you were loud at some points."

He had to fix this. "I think you're right. I'll call her and tell her to stop."

Her hysterical laugh drew the driver's attention in the rear-view mirror.

A deep frown replaced her joyless laughter. "Have you heard the same stories about her that I have? Crashing cars while drunk driving and not being punished. Getting people fired from their job because they didn't serve her fast enough? The woman is a holy terror who can get away with anything because her father is a billionaire."

She slumped into the seat. "She's delusional enough to think that you're her man. After what you told me,

I know it's not true, but still … The woman wants you and is willing to threaten me to have you."

"But she can't have me. I've told her that several times, and I'll do so again as soon as we get to my room." Fearful that Lamisi would give up on their new relationship before it even got started, he gripped her hands. "This is the last time she'll threaten you. I won't allow it to happen again."

"How can you stop her? She's money and power. That combination means she can do whatever she wants no matter who it hurts without consequences. God knows what she has planned for my dissertation. Not only have I had three advisors, but my current one already stalled me several times out of spite. If Deola whispers into his ear, I may never get my doctorate."

Lamisi bowed her head and rubbed her temples.

"I can't give up my dream, Blaise. I've worked too hard to get here, and I refuse to get pulled back." She raised her head and held his gaze. "By anyone."

A heaviness settled in his chest at her ominous words.

The taxi came to a halt. He looked out the window to find that they'd arrived at the hotel. Discussing how to handle Deola ranked high on the schedule for tonight. Just as Lamisi wasn't willing to jeopardize getting her PhD, he wouldn't lose her.

CHAPTER TWENTY-SIX

Lamisi's hand trembled as she pulled the cab's handle to let herself out while Blaise paid the driver. She'd been off-kilter ever since reading the horrible message. Melanie had pulled her to the side and asked what was wrong. She'd claimed nerves about being so close to the end of her dissertation.

And now, she'd confronted Blaise. His offer to talk to Deola was sweet, yet ridiculous. Whatever the woman wanted, she got, not matter who suffered in her acquirement of it. Was he strong enough to withstand Deola's wrath if he got in her way?

Doubt lingered as she waited for him to join her on the short path into the hotel. When he'd caught up with her, a man wearing a dark hoodie jogged towards them.

The guy called out, "Here's your lesson, bitch!"

Within the blink of an eye, he untwisted a bottle and aimed it.

In slow motion, liquid squirted towards her face and splattered before she could raise her hands to protect herself. She pushed out a scream just before Blaise ran and tackled the guy to the ground.

Their rolling scuffle didn't take long as she yelled at the anticipated burning of her face from the acid the man had sprayed her with. She would be scarred for life. Her howls brought people sprinting out of the hotel.

"Lamisi," Blaise said, out of breath. "Are you okay?"

He tugged at her wrists to bring her hands down from her face.

"Madam, what happened?" One of the hotel's attendants squatted next to her and asked in French.

Lamisi gulped in the cool air that hit her skin. Where was the sizzling agony of flesh melting that should've had her writhing on the ground? With gentle fingers, she tentatively touched her cheek where the fluid had landed. No pain. No caustic smell of chemicals. Nothing but moisture.

Heart racing, she looked at Blaise while answering the attendant.

"My face. He threw liquid at it." She swallowed hard. "Is it … disfigured?"

Brows furrowed together, Blaise took out his phone and turned on the flashlight. She squinted at the beam of light as he assessed her. "Not at all. Are you feeling any pain?"

She slumped and let out a sob of relief. It hadn't been acid in the bottle. Whatever it had been, she needed to wash it off. Struggling to get to her feet, she fell as her knees buckled. Blaise helped her up.

"Bathroom."

He assisted her inside with an entourage of gossiping hotel workers and a few guests following. He insisted on getting her into her room. Rather than wait for the elevator, she took the stairs two by two. Her hands too shaky to slip the key card into the slot, he took it and opened the door.

Sprinting in, she tore into the bathroom, stripped off her clothes, and rinsed her face.

Siphoning in a deep breath, she gathered courage to look into the mirror. She clutched the sink to keep from sliding to the floor when unmarred skin reflected back at her. Gratitude filled her chest. The back of her hand to her lips stifled the wail of relief that shook her body.

Not knowing what had been squirted at her, she dragged her crying self into the shower. Her nearly full bottle of face soap didn't hold enough for the number of times she scrubbed her face, neck, and chest. So she continued with her body soap.

A knock against the barrier startled her.

"Lamisi, are you okay?"

She swallowed back her tears and palmed the tiled wall for support.

"Yes," she choked out as the water continued to stream down her face.

Air ruffled the shower curtain as the door opened. His voice reached her ears clearer although he hadn't entered. "Are you sure? We should go to the hospital to have you checked out."

The last place she ever wanted to be. "No ... no hospital. I'm fine. I think it was only water the guy shot at me."

"Not acid?"

"No."

"Are you sure? We should still get to the emergency room to confirm."

"My face isn't burning. If it had been acid, the skin would have become warped."

"But what if—"

"I'm fine." The ferocity in the words bounced off the shower walls. Taking in a shaky breath, she spoke at a reasonable level around the lump that had formed in her throat. "Give me a while. I want to make sure to wash off whatever he got on me. You should do the same."

Seconds ticked by, and she feared he wouldn't leave.

"My door is open if you need anything. I'll be right back."

As soon as she heard the closing click of the door, tears mixed with the water sluicing over her, the drain collecting the residue of the nightmare she'd just endured.

***

There was nothing Blaise could do for her at that point, so he limped to his room. The fight with the assailant had led to soreness in the ankle he'd injured on the mountain. He'd wanted to chase the guy down when he'd escaped his grip, but taking care of Lamisi had been more important.

Worried about her, he took a quick shower. Her "fine" hadn't sounded it at all. Who would be after being attacked? Thank God it wasn't acid. Not only her beautiful face would have been marred, but her whole life would've been affected. Her outgoing personality might've taken a huge hit.

Her strength of will would have gotten her through it, especially since he'd have stayed by her side the whole time. She meant more to him that being a pretty face. Her intelligence, sense of humour, huge heart, talent, and determination made her special. She brought a unique light to his world that hadn't been there until he'd met her. Scarring wouldn't frighten him away from someone so extraordinary.

He hopped out of the shower, dried off, got dressed in a pair of shorts and T-shirt, grabbed his phone, and left his room to rap on Lamisi's door.

The barricade between them cleared, with her on the other side of the open threshold. Eyes puffy and red, the sight of her both made his heart clench and had him sending up a prayer of gratitude that her face hadn't been disfigured.

"Can I come in?"

She swept a hand into the room.

He took in an area almost identical to his, varying with a colour scheme of light orange and cream. Fighting the need to wrap her up and hold her for the rest of the night, he lowered himself into the only chair as she sat on the edge of the bed. Space might be the best thing for her. For someone he was strongly attracted to, he really didn't know her all that well.

"How are you doing?"

She shrugged, and her lower lip quivered.

He sprang from the chair onto the bed and wound his arms around her. Her tears poured onto his shoulder until her sobbing transitioned into intermittent shuddering breaths and sniffles.

She pushed herself up and walked across the room to grab the box of tissues. After blowing her nose, she kept her head bowed. Needing to soothe her, he went over and rubbed her back.

"Do you want to go to the police?"

"Ha. And say what? That a guy called me a bitch before squirting me with water? I can hear them having a big laugh and saying, 'Madam, when we have murders to solve, you expect us to care about this bit of nonsense?' just like they would in Ghana. No, thanks."

She had it right on point.

The guilt hit him once again. His association with Deola had caused this misery for Lamisi. "I'm sorry this happened to you."

He pulled out his phone from the cargo pocket of his shorts.

She grabbed his arm, her eyes glimmering. "Who are you calling?"

If it was the last thing he ever did, Blaise would make Deola pay for what she'd done. But first, to flush out her informant.

"There's only one way Deola could have known where I was and who I was with."

"You believe me that she's responsible?"

"Yes."

She closed her eyes for a second, inhaled so that her chest and shoulders rose, and nodded. "I wasn't sure if you would. I have no real proof."

"Your instincts are good enough for me."

"Thanks."

He hit send on Abdul's contact and waited. He would've never thought his friend would betray him.

Abdul's smiling face popped up on the screen when he answered. "Hey, man. How's Franco land treating you?"

Blaise held back a growl. "Lamisi got attacked. What the fu—"

She pinched his side.

He clenched his jaw, rubbed his chin, and counted to three. "Tell me what you know about it."

Mouth slackened, Abdul blinked several times while craning his neck closer to the phone. "*Me ya faru?*"

The Hausa flew naturally out of his mouth.

Blaise narrowed his eyes. Abdul had done a great job at looking confused, but he wasn't buying it. "You know what happened. And speak English."

"I don't know what you're talking about. What happened to Lamisi? Is she okay?"

"Someone has been harassing her over the phone, and tonight, they threw acid in her face."

Lamisi clutched his arm and squeezed.

"That's terrible. How is she?"

Blaise ignored the question. "You're the only one I told about my trip to Côte d'Ivoire with Lamisi.

You're the only one who could have told the attacker where we are."

Abdul gave a fierce shake of the head with a hand over his chest, as if swearing like they used to do as children. "I told no one of your trip."

Blaise assessed his friend's mannerisms with a critical eye. "Are you sure?"

"I promise on all that I hold dear that I told no one. I would never betray you, my brother."

Either Abdul had been taking acting lessons from top actors in Nollywood, or he was telling the truth. If that was the case, then how did Deola find them?

"I believe him," Lamisi whispered.

He gave a single nod of both acknowledgement and agreement. "Then how could Deola have known where we were?"

Eyes once again as round as clay bowls, Abdul's mouth dropped open. "You believe Deola did it?"

"Yes. She called me last night reminding me about the music awards. When I insisted that we weren't going together, she mentioned Lamisi."

Abdul set his mouth in scowl and waggled his finger. "I told you she wasn't a good person. I could sense it in her. Besides, young rich people who don't work for their money have too many issues. That one especially. Alima is always telling me that Deola is misunderstood, but I don't believe her. Being spoiled is never a good thing."

Blaise's spine straightened at the mention of Abdul's younger second wife. A memory niggled in the back of his mind but refused to clarify itself.

"Alima speaks highly of Deola. When Salifa or I contest her opinion on the woman, she becomes outraged. If I didn't know that they've never met, I would figure Alima to be a friend of hers."

A revelation announced itself in Blaise's head louder than the call to prayer. "When I told you about my trip to Côte d'Ivoire, I remember Alima hovering behind you."

He hadn't thought anything of it because the favoured wife was always around her husband.

It took Abdul a few seconds to make the connection before he bellowed out her name.

Alima jogged into view.

Lamisi leaned closer to Blaise so that her face was in the small section at the bottom of the screen. "She's the one who kept shooting me dirty looks and whispering while glaring at me at the hospital the day we met."

When Alima looked to the screen and noticed the faces staring at her, she narrowed her gaze and emitted, "*Karuwa*."

The word whore couldn't have been meant for Blaise.

"Alima! What has gotten into you, spitting out insults as if raised in the gutter? Apologize." Abdul had switched to Hausa since the woman didn't speak English as fluently as his first wife.

With militant defiance, she folded her arms so viciously under her breasts that it pulled at her hijab. "I will not."

"Why not, Alima?" Blaise asked on a tone much kinder than the one he wanted to dish out. He would play good cop today. "Has Lamisi offended you?"

"Yes." Spitting with indignation, she continued. "By trying to steal you from my friend, she has become my enemy."

Guilty. It wouldn't hurt to get more evidence. "Who is Lamisi trying to steal me from?"

"Deola. You have agreed to marry her. She has told me that the announcement will be made at the music awards where you two have planned a public proposal. My friend has told me all of the details." She sighed. "Very romantic." Her eyes sharpened with a flick towards Lamisi. "She will not ruin it. You belong with Deola."

The occupants in both rooms stilled with silence and confusion.

"I'm not marrying Deola," Blaise shouted. The woman had gone too far.

"How are you and Deola friends?" Abdul asked at the same time.

Alima grinned at her husband. "She responded to me when I left a message on her page a few months ago when Blaise and she initially met. I was proud that Blaise had finally met a woman worthy of him."

At least, she'd had his best interest at heart. It still didn't dispel the anger keeping him on the cusp of crashing his phone against the wall.

Lamisi rested a hand on his upper thigh.

"Did you tell Deola that Blaise had travelled to Abidjan?"

"Yes. We are the best of friends and talk about many things." The young woman's smile lit her face. "When she asks about Blaise, I inform her. She always takes my calls. She was pleased with me when I told her about your weekend trip to Abidjan." Alima shot daggers from her eyes at Lamisi. "Even if it was with *her*."

Lamisi's low growl hit his ears, but didn't reach the phone's speaker. He had no doubt that blood would be shed if the women were in the same room.

"You have not done well," Abdul chastised in a strict tone, leaving no doubt that Alima would learn the error of her ways. "Leave me."

Alima opened her mouth as if to protest, but then seemed to think better of it when she looked into her husband's scowling countenance. She scurried away.

Blaise had heard more than enough. He returned to English. "I'm sorry I blamed you, my friend."

"No worries, Blaise." Abdul averted his gaze to meet Lamisi's eyes before bowing his head. "I apologize for the actions of my wife. I assure you that it will never happen again." The screen filled with his face. "I'm glad you weren't injured."

"Thank you."

Blaise turned to look at Lamisi's profile at her softly spoken words devoid of any irritation. Her features no longer held the tension they had just moments ago. Could she have truly forgiven that quickly? He knew that she had when she turned and her dark brown eyes caught his gaze and held.

He was honoured to have met such a remarkable woman.

Abdul cleared his throat.

Resistant to lose the link he had with Lamisi, it took him longer than it should have to return his attention back to the screen. He entwined their fingers to keep the connection.

His friend rubbed his full beard. "What will you do about Deola? The woman is crazier than I thought."

"That's a fact. I'll talk to her. By the end of the conversation, I know she will back down."

Abdul raised a brow, but didn't ask any further questions. Once again, he gave a slight bow to Lamisi. "I am truly sorry for the stress you have suffered and my wife's role in it."

He must really be feeling the guilt to elicit two apologies.

"*Na yarda da uzuri.*" Lamisi accepted the apology in Hausa, revealing that she held no ill will towards Abdul.

"Just make sure she understands that what she did is wrong," Blaise added. "My business is no one else's but my own."

"Yes. I'll talk to you later, my friend. Have a good night, Lamisi."

"You, too."

The screen went blank with the cut call.

Blaise pinched the bridge of his nose and released a mouth full of air, glad that his friend hadn't betrayed him. Now to shake Deola from his life.

CHAPTER TWENTY-SEVEN

Over the shock of being assaulted, a wild hunger of fury took its place. Abdul's idiot wife wasn't the one to blame. Deola was.

No matter what Blaise said to her, nothing would change. The woman with the kind of power and money Lamisi couldn't even fathom would come after her again. And again. The prima donna wanted Blaise, and there was probably nothing she wouldn't do in order to make it happen.

Scenes from too many Nigerian and Ghanaian movies where a woman was kidnapped by a jealous ex came to mind. The ideas had to be initiated from somewhere. She had no doubt that Deola could and would make her disappear without getting caught.

Was she willing to risk her life for a man? Not just any man, but Blaise. The one her heart seemed to beat for. They hadn't known each other for long, but he was so comfortable to be around that she had no difficulty being her true self. That had to mean something.

Didn't it?

No one else could live for her. Being with Blaise would be a wonderful experience, but she came first. If she were to continue down a path of having a relationship with him, she would live in a constant state of fear. Watching over her shoulder, waiting to be attacked from any and all directions. What kind of life would that be even if she were with the man that made her feel amazing and special?

Their romance had to end even before it had started. Yet, she couldn't leave him without experiencing what they could have been together. She would have no regrets about leaving him. But first ...

Bolder than she'd ever behaved, she looked into his eyes and closed the space between them. Mouths met with zips of electrical charges. At the slight parting of her lips, he deepened the kiss.

His solid muscles beneath her hands flexed as she caressed his back and pressed closer. Not close enough to satisfy. Everything disappeared at the onslaught of their explosive passion. Consequences no longer existed, only the pleasure they could experience. Together.

With the acceptance that this night would be their first and last together, Lamisi released all inhibitions and pulled Blaise with her when she lowered onto her back.

He released her lips. Panting, he stared down at her. "Lamisi?"

He'd given her the time to back out. She wouldn't. The moment went beyond anything she had ever experienced. She longed for him more than even her next breath. She raised her leg to hook around his hip.

"Make love to me, Blaise."

Brows arched over eyes that held her bound and mesmerized. "Are you sure?"

If tonight had left her one lesson, it was that life was worth living right now.

She reached up to smooth a hand over his cheek. He was her present. Nothing else mattered. A nod of affirmation later, his lips crashed down onto hers, permeating her with the slick heat of his mouth. The spiciness of his scent and the pressure of his muscular body on top of hers—he filled her with a desire so strong that any concept of regret became inconceivable.

He lifted himself off the bed, leaving her skin cool and wanting, and reached his hands down. When she clasped them, he tugged her to her feet.

With a deliberateness that she'd only experienced in her fantasies with him, he stripped off her clothes, trailing kisses and suckling sensitized flesh as he exposed her.

As he removed his clothes in a more hurried manner, Lamisi's practical side kicked in. On wobbly legs, she went to her bag and pulled out an unopened box of condoms. Thank God for a best friend who worked in healthcare and had insisted that she buy them.

She pivoted to face him. The box slipped from her fingers when sumptuous chocolate skin covering lean muscle met her gaze. She picked up the condoms and reached out for him. Her hands smoothed over the light dusting of coily hair on a solid chest and rippled over his defined abdomen.

Before she could reach her target, he grabbed her wrists and brought them up to his mouth. The light graze of his lips at the sensitive areas just below her palms sent tingles down her spine and moist heat to her core.

He held her arms away from her body and looked her up and down with a glint in his eyes. "Lamisi, you're gorgeous."

Foregoing any kind of shyness, she returned the favour over his body. "You, too."

Blaise moved to her, and they touched skin to skin from chest to thighs.

"Are you sure?" he repeated.

His warm breath over her ear sent a shiver through her.

More than she was of anything she had ever done in her life. "Yes."

He removed the box from her hold, ripped it open, and took out a single packet. Lamisi stood motionless as he opened it and slid it over his rigid length.

A shadow passed over as the reality of the moment invaded. This one-night experience would have to last her for the rest of her life.

She led him to the bed and tugged him down with her. Fingers stroked intimate places. Lips and tongues caressed as kisses drove their unyielding hunger.

When their bodies joined, she knew their souls had, too. Their oneness became her world as they moved together in gratifying strokes.

Stars exploded behind her eyes as her climax took her to the heavens and beyond. Blaise called out her name with his explosion within her a moment later.

They lay entwined for the longest time. He kissed her shoulder before getting out of bed and heading towards the bathroom.

Lamisi covered her naked body with the sheet as questions bombarded her. Two stood out as the most prominent. Why did she miss him so much when he was close enough to throw a shoe at the door he'd just walked behind? The second tore at her heart—did she have to let him go?

After their spectacular love making, she felt even closer to him on all levels. Her skin tingled, and blood pulsed at the recent memory. What they had shared couldn't be considered normal. More like destined. Dare she even think it when she wasn't sure she believed in it?

Shadows silhouetted Blaise as he came out of the bathroom. He eased onto the bed and hovered over her. The sweet kisses to her lips as his body pressed against hers teased.

He settled a pillow under his head, facing her profile, and sighed as if he were the most content man in the world. It made sense since she was flying high herself.

"What will you do when you finish your dissertation?"

She snapped her head to the side to catch his gaze. Not what she'd expected.

"I figured I'd continue on the road to professorship at the University of Ghana. Ever since I was young, people considered me to be strange because I understood so many languages. When I went to the university, I stood out in an impressive way, and it suited me. Things got even better when I started working as a teaching assistant. I loved it.

"The combination of teaching, researching, and being around like-minded people who live, not just speak, languages as much as me is my ideal job. It would allow me to travel and encounter other cultures and languages, as well."

His refined nose crinkled, and she raised herself onto her elbow to see him better in the semi darkness.

"What?"

The shoulder closest to her shrugged. "Speaking as one of your students, you're a fantastic teacher, and I can see you imparting your knowledge in the classroom."

"And doing research," she added.

"Okay."

"But ..." she filled in for him.

"You're so gifted with languages that I can see you doing a lot more."

The follicles on her head tingled in recognition of the concept. Hearing something voiced that she had thought herself renewed the longing she'd once had about travelling the world. Maybe writing a book. Helping people in some way.

"Like what?"

His gaze held hers. "Working for the UN or something along those lines. Going international rather than being local. Doing something where your ability will be appreciated and praised."

"You don't think that will happen if I teach at Legon?"

He stroked a hand down her arm, sending sparks of heat along the limb. "With the title of doctor, you'll be respected anywhere in Ghana, but will your talents be fully utilized?"

Lamisi followed her impulse to brush her nose against his cheek and inhaled his spicy, musky scent.

"Thank you," she whispered against the hair on his cheek.

"For what?" His voice came out on a husky groan.

"Seeing so much in me."

Blaise elevated himself onto his elbow, separating them for a moment until he cupped her cheek. "I like everything I've discovered about you. I'm sure that the more I find out about you, the more amazed I'll become."

She leaned in with a brush of lips that transitioned into a sweet encounter of love making.

This time, when he left her satiated body, the loss caused a crushing in her chest, representing more than just their physical separation.

CHAPTER TWENTY-EIGHT

An insistent vibration and pinging woke Lamisi from sleep. The morning sun streamed through a crack in the curtains when she opened her eyes. The heft of Blaise's arm blanketing her kept her in place. It had been the best night of her life. No regrets lingered.

The buzzing of her phone demanded that she leave their cocoon. When she shifted, he groaned and pulled her closer. The annoying vibration on the dresser wouldn't allow her to snuggle in. By the frequency of the dinging, someone urgently needed her.

Her heart picked up its pace as a number of nasty scenarios rampaged into her mind of the people she cared about being injured.

The phone shook with more incoming messages even as she picked it up. Lamisi slid her finger across the numbers which would unlock her screen.

Thirty-four messages. And more coming in. Did she want to open them? The prickly sensation and goose bumps on her arms said no.

"What's going on?"

She let out a screech. Whirling, she placed a hand against her chest as she gulped in air.

"Sorry. I didn't mean to frighten you."

Blaise's raspy voice reminded her of the first time they'd spoken, and her stomach flipped.

"It's okay."

He pointed at the still vibrating phone. "Is there a problem?"

A glance down at the device indicated that she now had a total of forty-five messages. "It's blowing up with messages. I think it's Deola."

The muscle in his jaw clenched. "I should've called her last night to tell her to cut it out."

Her core pulsed at the memory of what they'd shared. Nothing had ever made her feel so alive and connected with another person. For the rest of her life, she'd cherish having been with him.

Lamisi focused on her phone and tapped on her message button. She gasped as she noticed that the messages were from different numbers. TrueCaller had identified none of them. What had the insane woman done?

Swallowing her fear, she looked through the titles of the messages without having to open a single one. Each message held one word as she scanned down. The total message repeated until the phone came to its fill.

'Leave. Him. Alone. Otherwise. Next. Time.'

Hands shaking, she drew on her courage. Daring to open one text revealed the same singular word which had been in the title. When she opened the next six, they all held one word.

The next set of phone numbers were different. So were the next. And the next. Just like the guy who had sprayed her, Deola had gotten people to do her dirty work for her.

Eyes glued to the screen, she shook her head in disbelief. "She's certifiable!"

"I'm calling her right now." Blaise's tone held a level of rage that sent a chill down her spine. "This will stop."

A snort ripped out of her. "What good will that do? The woman wants you, and nothing will stop her."

Certain defeat hit her where only moments ago she'd held hope. She'd known it last night. Wasn't that why she'd made love to him? To experience being with him for one night. Their first and last time together.

'*Next time...*'

Would Deola attack her family? Friends?

Lamisi couldn't risk it, no matter how much she cared about Blaise. She had too much to live for to let another woman destroy her or anyone she loved.

"Once I talk to Deola—" Blaise broke into her thoughts, "—she'll understand that she and I aren't and never will be a couple. Ever."

Lamisi swallowed the lump in her throat. They had met less than a month ago. Why should letting him go hurt so much?

"She'll keep coming after me until I'm out of the picture so she can have you for herself."

Blaise tapped his chest. "She can't have me. Once I let her know definitively, she'll back off."

"Right. Just like she did the times you told her before."

"This will be differ—"

She flung up a hand. "Yes, it will. I won't be in her way. Blaise, I can't do this. It would be stupid for me to think I can ever escape her. She has too much money and influence, and knows how to use it to get what she wants."

"No, Lamisi. You are not breaking up with me. Not over this. We're good together, and you know it. I'm not just talking about in bed."

Boy, did she know. Unable to look into his earnest eyes, she spun and paced to the window. Commuters on their way to wherever they needed to be greeted her blurred vision.

Hands on her shoulders seeped a warmth into her that she couldn't resist. Lamisi rested her back against him. Making her choose between herself and Blaise was cruel.

He wound his arms around her and rested his chin against her shoulder. Their cheeks pressed, and she closed her eyes, breathing him in. This was where she belonged. In a perfect world, she would be able to stay.

She jumped as the shrill sound of her phone broke into her longing. Would her cell going off be a perpetual cause for fear? It would if she stayed with Blaise. Always looking over her shoulder wasn't the way she wanted to live. Not the way anyone should have to live.

"My alarm." She tore herself away from him to turn it off. "We need to get ready to leave so we don't miss our flight."

"Lamisi, we can work this out. Trust me. Deola will back off."

She tilted her head and took in his stunning features. Dark eyes stared back with a softness that spoke of the pleading that hadn't come from his mouth.

"When I was ten, I almost died. Typhoid fever created a hole in my gut. I had an emergency operation." She rubbed her arms to ward off the chill that came over her. "After the surgery, my wound got infected. I spent weeks in the hospital being poked, prodded, and in so much pain that I'm sure nothing could come close to it."

He blinked at her as if wondering the purpose of the story.

"I hate hospitals. I don't use that word for anything else but hospitals. Passing by them freaks me out. It takes an impossible amount of coaxing for me to go into one."

"You went in with me when I sprained my ankle."

"Yes."

"You liked me even back then."

Yes. But that wasn't the point.

"Whatever Deola has in store for me will not end well. You're a good man, and I've enjoyed getting to know you, but I have to think of myself first. Life is too valuable."

The sentiment she'd spewed came nowhere near what she truly felt, but if he knew that he possessed her heart, he'd become vigilant in his attempt to persuade her to stay with him. She was barely hanging on to her decision as it stood. No matter what convincing argument he came up with, she knew that walking out of this hotel in any kind of relationship with him would put her in danger. Her life mattered too much.

"I care about you, Lamisi. Give us a chance. We'll get through this and come out stronger for it."

Such a romantic. She'd miss that about him.

Rather than reject his offer, she took the couple of steps separating them, cupped his face, and raised herself to kiss his lips. Just like when they'd made love, she took in all of him, understanding, even if he didn't, that it would be their last time together.

CHAPTER TWENTY-NINE

"Your French has improved tremendously," Armand told Blaise as they walked to the front door after their tutorial.

Blaise had noticed that the man no longer looked pained after his pupil had spoken.

"*Merci.*"

He didn't bother to explain about his journey to Côte d'Ivoire or how Lamisi had forced him to speak the language with everyone they'd encountered during the trip. The weekend had been a blast. Until it no longer had been.

They'd gone from having a slow relationship to taking off on a rocket. Being with her had been mind-blowing. Soul-shaking. Incredible.

His attempts to contact Deola had yielded three days of beeping in his ear with a computerized female voice stating that the phone had been switched off. He'd even had Alima try from her phone. Nothing.

Either Deola was ignoring him, or the oil rig she was supposedly on had no reception. Yet, she'd been able to contact him, organize an assault and an army of texters to harass Lamisi. His money was on her avoiding him.

He had spoken to Lamisi for a few short minutes each day. He could understand her perspective. He would've flipped out if someone had made him the target of their vengeance.

It had been a long time since he'd met a woman who matched and challenged him. He'd fight for her. Since it meant taking on Deola, then that's what he'd do. And he'd win.

Frustrated, he called the strongest woman he knew for advice.

"Hello, my son," his mother said in Hausa, the only language she spoke with her children even though she was also fluent in English and Twi.

An involuntary smile spread across his face. There wasn't a woman he'd ever loved more. "Hi, Mama."

In many ways, he considered her to be his best friend. He wouldn't take the step and talk about sex with her, but the topic of women was another issue. And she tended to share wise advice about them.

"The trip to Côte d'Ivoire was successful. I'm more fluent in speaking French."

"Anything you set your mind to, you achieve. You are my and your father's son, so it is must be so."

The woman knew how to encourage. Just like Lamisi. He stood and paced the room. May as well get everything out in the open.

"I've found a woman that I like."

"I knew I'd heard a change in your voice. More melodic. Who is she? I'm sure she's a good Muslim girl, if you're telling me about her."

"Lamisi Imoro. Yes, she's a Muslim." He'd leave out the fact that she wasn't as devoted as his mother would like her to be. "She's studying for her PhD in linguistics at the University of Ghana. She's the one who helped me translate my lyrics into French."

"She's going to be a doctor?" Her words came out breathy with excitement. "*And* she's Muslim. Praise be to Allah for answering this mother's prayers for her child. Allah is ever faithful. You have just made me the happiest mother in all of Ghana. When are you bringing her here to introduce her? What tribe is she? Is she educated? What work do her parents do?"

He tapped a hand against his chest to ensure that he'd survived the rapid fire of questions. "Mama, I only met her a month ago, and we're getting to know each other."

"You don't have the answers?"

"She speaks eight languages. One of them is Hausa."

His mother gasped. "Is she Hausa like us?"

"No, Mama. Her mother is Dagomba, she works for the Ministry of Agriculture, and her father is Ga. He owns his own business."

He chuckled at her squeals and claps.

"She's a Northerner *and* a Muslim. You have delighted my heart this day. I must meet her. Put her on the screen right now so we can talk. I'm hanging up."

"Wait, Mama." He caught her before she could disconnect the call.

"Yes."

"She's not here."

"Well, go get her. Call me back when you have."

Sometimes, there was nothing as frustrating as speaking to the queen aspect of his mother.

"I have a problem I need your help with." The words would capture her.

"What is it, son?"

"Deola."

Was that a growl on her end?

"I told you to stay away from her. She may be Muslim, but from her pictures, I could sense her evil heart."

He would've doubted it before, but after what she did to Lamisi, he knew it to be a fact. He told the story of Deola's treachery.

"I know why she doesn't want to release you. You're talented, rich, popular, and come from a royal and influential home. If that wasn't enough, you are loyal, kind-hearted, and generous. More than you should be at times. No woman would ever want to let that go."

Except Lamisi. Extenuating circumstances in a new relationship didn't count.

"What do I do?"

"First of all, be patient with Lamisi. She has every right to protect herself. As for Deola, keep trying to get in contact with her and let her know where you stand." His mother paused. "What makes you sure that she'll stop disturbing Lamisi once you've spoken to her?"

His mother wouldn't appreciate that he'd threaten her with information he knew she wouldn't want to get out to the public.

"I'll appeal to her better judgment," he answered.

"She has none, but do what you feel is best. As for Lamisi, give her time. Maybe invite her to the music awards. We're proud of you for all your nominations, especially Artiste of the Year."

His bowed his head even though she couldn't see. He always wanted to bring honour to the family. "Thank you, Mama. It's been a long, challenging journey. Lamisi is a private woman. This wouldn't be the best time to introduce her to the world. And until I clear things up with Deola, I feel as if Lamisi will stay away from me."

"It's what I would do," she said. "In the meantime, stay in contact with her. And if you can, keep her safe."

"Thank you for the advice."

"I hope you take it this time. Now tell me more about Lamisi."

He spent the rest of the conversation talking about his new favourite topic. By the end of the conversation, he felt like he knew more about Lamisi than he'd initially thought. He'd pulled out facts he hadn't realized he'd known. Perhaps he shouldn't have shared it all with his mother, but his tongue had been too loose to rein in.

He grinned at the fact that he was hung up enough over a woman to share the news with his mother. Now if he could get Lamisi to feel the same about him.

***

Lamisi had spent the past week and a half in a pseudo-state of boredom while transcribing the musicians' interview responses. Thoughts of Blaise creeping in led to the work being even more tedious, because she'd lose track of what the artists had said and would have to rewind the recording so she could type it in on her computer.

At least being in the house didn't cause her to tremble like the few times she'd had to venture out. By the time she returned to the safety of her home, she'd collapse onto the couch. Her muscles had protested the tension she'd suffered while paying such close attention to her surroundings. Yet, she refused to let anything, even being terrified that Deola would stage another attack, limit her life.

Her family had wanted to call the police and find every way to contact Deola once she'd told them what had happened. She'd reasoned them out of it, but warned them to be careful. It didn't feel like enough.

Lamisi sent up prayers that the heiress would understand that she no longer had any intention of seeing Blaise and back off.

The impulse to drive to his house because she missed him so fiercely was almost more than she could stand at times. She'd lunge onto the phone when the ringtone she'd assigned him pierced the air. Hearing his voice, even for the few moments she allowed so she could wean herself from him, gave her respite.

Her parents had taught her how to face her fears from a very young age, and here she was cowering in her own life. It wasn't like her to hide from anything but a hospital.

Giving up what she desired most wasn't like her, either, and it hurt to go against her natural instinct to cling to the man who'd filled her heart. Soon, she'd have to sever all ties with Blaise. Give it an official end so she could start to heal and move on.

As if that would ever happen.

CHAPTER THIRTY

Lamisi hadn't warmed up to him after their return from Côte d'Ivoire. In fact, she was drawing farther away every day. Not even the offer of a drive on his motorcycle had gotten him closer to seeing her.

Along with their daily phone calls, he'd sent her several poetic text messages, hoping she'd read them. That his smooth words would melt the ice she'd built around her. So far, they hadn't. At least, she hadn't cut him off completely.

His phone rang as he paced the pathway in his garden.

"Hello, Bizzy."

Deola's face filled the screen, as beautiful as ever. Only now did he see the tinge of ugliness within her.

"Hello, Deola." He kept his tone dull and looked her in the eyes. No further formalities needed, he dove right in. "I know you were the one who had Lamisi Imoro attacked in Abidjan and have been harassing her."

Red, glossy lips rounded as her extended lashes fluttered with each blink. "I have no idea what you're talking about. I've been on that oil rig, remember. It wasn't as bad as I thought it would be. Aside from a lack of consistent network connection, it had all the comforts of home. The food——"

"Stop lying. We all know you're responsible."

Deola's eyes narrowed. "According to whom? The woman who is after you for your money and fame? What do you even see in her, Bizzy? She's a local lowlife who isn't destined for any type of greatness. She can't help you rise to the top or be the best in the business. Not like I can."

And there it was. His fist flexed into a fist that needed to make contact with a solid surface. Other than a clenched jaw, he kept his expression neutral and his mouth shut so she could dig herself in deeper.

She raked multicolour-painted acrylic nails through the hair of her wig.

"I don't ever want you to say that I didn't warn you. She can't do anything for you but put you into debt with her poverty-driven spending." Her voice rose with her temper. "I realized it from the first time I saw footage of her at your house. Wearing cheap clothes and hugging you as if she were a whore."

"What are you talking about?"

"She's a gold digger. Before you know it, your money will be gone and your career destroyed," she said with bared upper teeth in a vicious snarl.

She was delusional if she thought he'd let go of what she'd let slip. He squinted, staring into her the eyes. "What did you mean by footage, Deola?"

She flipped down a hand in dismissal.

"Nothing. Something I said in annoyance," she said in a higher pitched voice with a smile meant to distract. "But can you please take my advice to heart? I care about you."

He replayed the sentence and the words *at your house* hit him. Would she have had the gall to do it? After what Deola had put Lamisi through, nothing should surprise him about the lengths she was willing to go to get what she wanted.

He clicked off the phone and sprinted out of his backyard until he reached the front of his house.

Turning, he scanned his roof. Nothing.

The gate gave a slight creak as he opened it. He ignored his ringing phone while perusing the roofs of the homes across the street.

The camera on the house two plots down caught his eye. When had they put up a security camera? The couple who owned the place had travelled to the States a few months ago, informing him that they'd left their son alone while he attended university. They hadn't mentioned anything about installing a security camera.

Jogging across the street, he assessed the home for more cameras. None.

Rather than bang his fist against the metal, he poked his finger into the doorbell. A young man opened the gate, wearing a wide smile.

"Yo, Bizzy. How's it going, man?"

He held out a hand that Blaise grasped and slid his palm across his before they ended the connection with a snap.

"I'm great, Felix. How're you doing?"

"Living the life. Catching up on sleep now that exams are done."

"*Abeg*. Did your parents have a security system put in?"

Felix tapped his chest with his thumb and chuckled. "I'm their security. They like doing things the old-fashioned way. Why?"

Blaise pointed to the roof. "What's that?"

Felix rotated, took a look, and then stepped closer to the camera. "What the hell is that?"

"You've never seen it before?"

"Nope. Never. Look how it's tucked under the roof's edge."

Blaise nodded. "If you didn't look up, you wouldn't see it. Who looks up at the roof unless it's leaking?"

"How did you find it?"

His nostrils flared as he glared at the offensive technology. He'd never experienced such a violation of his privacy. Not even the paparazzi had the tenacity to have him watched. She had no right. "I was looking."

Felix pointed from the camera along its trajectory.

"Damn, *Chale*." He used the local slang for friend. "It looks like someone's been watching your house."

Blaise tried to play it cool, even though his head was seconds away from exploding. "Yeah, seems that way."

The young man grinned. "Too bad they don't know how quiet you like to live for a hiplife artist. No off-the-chain parties for you."

Blaise shrugged. "It's not my scene, especially in my home."

"I get it."

He doubted it. People held a certain expectation of musicians. He didn't fit it.

"Listen, Felix, I'll make a couple of calls to get the camera taken down."

"No *wahala*. I'm around for the afternoon."

"Thanks, *Chale*."

Blaise stormed back to his home and contacted the guys who'd installed his home security system. They'd be there within the hour to investigate.

Stripping down to his boxer briefs in his backyard, he dove into the pool. The cool water didn't invigorate like it normally did. The laps he raced through did a better job of tamping down his rage.

Lifting himself out of the pool, he went to his clothes and dried his head, face, and hands on his shirt before slipping it on and picking up his phone.

"Hi, Blaise. What happened? I've been trying to call."

The sweetness of her voice irritated him to the point of wanting to throw the cell against the side of his home.

"You set up a camera on the house across the street from me."

Her eyes rounded. "What are you talking about?"

"Don't play with me, Deola. I have my security team coming right now. They've assured me that they'll be able to trace the signal to where it's transmitting." They'd said nothing of the sort, and he had no idea if it could be done, but he doubted she did, either. "You had it installed to spy on me."

"Come on, Blaise. Spy is such a harsh word. I only wanted to ensure your security."

He swiped a hand down his face and dragged in a breath through the palm he left over his mouth. "You're incredible. Stay the hell away from me and Lamisi."

"You don't belong with anyone but me." The venom returned. "That bitch can go to Hell."

No wonder Lamisi had wanted to stay as far away from him as possible. Deola was demented. He wouldn't put it past her to murder anyone who got in her way.

If only Lamisi knew how much of an upper hand he had, she would've had more faith in him.

Time to put an end to it.

"All I know is that you'd better leave her alone. If I find out that you've done anything to her, I'll be the one you have to answer to. Do you understand?"

Her laughter came out high and piercing. "Your kindness and innocence are two of the things I've always adored about you. You think you're going anywhere because you've found a side chick? Soon, you'll be begging me to restore your fame when your stupid French album tanks. And it will. Nigerians won't buy it, and they're all that matter in West Africa. English is the way to go. We tolerate your Ghanaian local languages because your beats are so catchy."

"Enough!" he barked out.

Her head snapped back. No one dared to speak to the heiress in such a manner.

"Do you remember the time you insisted that I spend the weekend in one of your guest rooms instead of a hotel?" Blaise asked.

"Yes. My dad was out of town. It was the night you kissed me."

Funny how he remembered her throwing herself at him.

"I had difficulty sleeping on Saturday night and went exploring through your massive home in search of the kitchen."

An ashiness replaced the make-up induced glow of her skin.

"I heard muffled screams and the sound of slaps coming from the room tucked around the corner of the first-floor hallway. Not knowing if you were in danger, I opened the door." He shook his head. "I always wondered why you hadn't locked it. Were you too excited about your activities, or did you want me to discover you?" He raised a brow. "Maybe join you? And your, um, friends."

She wiggled in her seat. "I ... I ... don't know what you're talking about."

"S&M isn't my thing."

He ignored her gasp.

"When I saw that you were safe and rather happy wearing your leather while wielding a whip on your poor, um, friends, I closed the door and left. Scarred with the image of the supposed virgin heiress partaking in—"

"You're lying. That never happened. I would never do such a thing."

"No?"

Strands of hair flew into her face with her vehement head shake.

"You want to degrade my name. It won't work, Blaise. Everyone knows I don't involve myself in scandalous behaviour. Especially not what you described." She let out a grunt of derision. "You'd better keep your fantasies to yourself. They don't reflect well on your wholesome brand."

He sat in the pool chair and anchored his free hand behind. "So the pictures I took won't stand as proof of your sadistic activities? Huh. Let's see what the public thinks about my evidence if you ever try to get in contact with or hurt Lamisi again. Don't think I won't bring you down in order to keep her safe."

"You're lying," she squeaked out. "What you're describing never happened."

He held her gaze. "You're known for your fashion sense, but bright pink leather doesn't look as good on you as you think. I give you props for the matching whip. Along with the spiked dog collar and leash you had on your other, um, friend."

The image on the screen flipped over and then went black as her phone landed face down. And then, the line went dead.

Blaise luxuriated in the knowledge that he'd won. Only a fool would challenge him. Several minutes ticked by as he lounged in the sun, waiting. When his phone rang, he turned on the recorder—he didn't doubt she'd done the same—before answering.

Deola tossed her hair over her shoulder, looking more in control than when he'd delivered the news.

"I have no idea what you're talking about, Blaise Zemar Ayoma." Deola enunciated his full name. He half expected her to add son of, throwing in his parents' names as proof to anyone who might listen to the recording in the future.

"About any of it," she continued. "I've been busy learning the family business and have been out of communication on an oil rig."

If he didn't know better, he would've believed her.

She released a deep sigh. "It's a pity your friend was attacked. The world is not the same as it once was."

"No, it isn't."

"Please give her my regards. I'll provide the poor dear with what you requested."

He dipped his head towards her in a sign of understanding. "With a reassurance that any such trauma will never come to her again would be helpful. You know how people look up to you and trust your word. If you say it won't ever happen again, then she'll believe that it never will."

Her contracted shoulders shortened her elegant neck. "I agree."

Lamisi would believe Deola's direct promise of leaving her alone.

"Thank you. There are certain things that will never come into public view because they're too painful."

"They should be deleted from all sources, never to be spoken of again."

"Yes. Just as some friendships should end, but cordiality maintained when running in the same circles."

She giggled, but her eyes remained cold. "Burning bridges serves no one. As always, it was lovely speaking with you, Bizzy. Take care of yourself."

"You, too, Deola."

When her face disappeared, his body went limp and the back of his head slammed into the wood of the chair. The relief of being rid of Deola outweighed the sting of pain.

Time to figure out how to convince Lamisi that they belonged together.

CHAPTER THIRTY-ONE

What had gotten into Blaise to make him send such romantic texts over the past few days? Every time she went to press the delete button, her finger spasmed in protest. She'd sighed with longing after rereading them at least twenty times each.

His words were too beautiful, reminding her more of poetry than messages.

One in particular had her heart racing.

'I am not worthy of such a blessing as her.
The woman of faith had me longing for more.
Light in her eyes, laughter from her mouth, kindness from her soul
Bring me to a state of need too great to contain.
My world has been thrown off course and a new path set.
It is with her that I see the future flow.'

She slid her finger across the screen to clear it. Time to stop moping about him and get on with life. His texts weren't enough to make her change her mind.

What would? her heart taunted.

Deola had contacted her and told her in a covert manner that she would back off. It didn't mean that she belonged with Blaise. If they got together, wouldn't some other woman who thought she deserved him more than Lamisi come and try to bump her off one day?

But then again, maybe she could be enough.

She'd never know unless she gave them a chance. Did she trust him enough with her heart to do that? Did she believe in herself?

She sank into her bed, ending the question and answer period in her overactive mind. Picking up the remote control, she turned on her television and switched to the station showing the music awards. They were still ushering people onto the red carpet, so she kept it on mute while watching the glamour pass by on her screen.

How many of the artists she'd interviewed would be at the ceremony?

Who was she kidding? She didn't care. She watched for one reason only. To catch a glimpse of the man who had shaken her world and caused her to question so many things about who she knew herself to be.

Whatever happened between them, she hoped Blaise won all the categories he'd been nominated for, especially Artiste of the Year. He deserved it. His competition consisted of some great musicians, but Blaise was the absolute best.

You only think that because you're in love with him.

She bounded out of bed, slapping a palm against her forehead. "Oh my goodness."

Dropping onto the edge of the mattress, she supported herself with braced arms so she wouldn't slide off.

Was she in love with him?

She wiggled her fingers, and prickles of numbness woke them. How long had she been contemplating her feelings about the man she'd tossed away out of fear and self-preservation?

Yes, she loved him. Unexpected and scary, but true.

What would she do about it? Love wasn't something that came into her life often. Precious would tell her to go for it. Should she, or was it too late? His texts didn't indicate it. Those treasurable words spoke of the opposite.

For the first time since she'd tried ghosting herself out of his life, she thought of Blaise and smiled. Her heart still hammered with uncertainty, but at least, she was willing to give them a chance.

A banging on her door jarred her out of her musings. "Come in."

Amadu burst in, glanced at the silent screen, and then grabbed the remote control. "You've got to see this."

Her breath caught as Blaise filled her screen.

Amadu turned the volume up. "He's singing a new song. In French, Twi, and English. Is it one of the ones you two were working on?"

As she listened, the lyrics sounded familiar, but the song hadn't been one she'd translated for him. She would definitely recall a tune that made her wind her hips while still seated. The music was slower than his previously released songs. Smoother.

After a few minutes, the impact of the words hit her, and she gravitated to the television.

"Damn!"

The lyrics were the same as the texts he'd sent her. Only instead of them being in English, he sang the chorus in impeccable French.

Amadu tugged her out of the way. "Yeah, he sounds amazing. I don't understand half of what he's saying, but the beat is killer."

The crowd seemed to think so, too, as they danced. Rotating their hips, showing off the strength of their thighs and asses. At least the ladies did. She expected at least one of them to injure herself with the extent of their movements. The men in the crowd didn't seem to mind as they watched with smiling appreciation.

Was she the only one who knew he was pouring his heart out? Did anyone else care that the lyrics could bring tears to their eyes if fully understood? Or was it just her?

She blinked away the burn.

And then, the camera focused on a woman with hair flowing over bare shoulders. An emerald green dress cascaded over her curvaceous body. Deola smiled wide with one hand against her chest as she blew a kiss to Blaise.

Lamisi's skin went cold with dread. She couldn't believe what she'd just witnessed. The two were together. They had to be. Why else was she at the event gazing at him like a woman enamoured? It had to be the reason why Deola had contacted her, because she'd won.

Like a scared sheep, Lamisi had walked out on him. Leaving him to fall in love with whoever his heart chose. It obviously wasn't her. She didn't blame him, either. The easy way out of a situation wasn't always the best. Now that she'd come to terms with her feelings for him, she wished she could've handled things differently. Trusted that he would take care of Deola like he said he would.

"Are you okay?" Amadu asked.

She forced a smile. "I'm fine. The song just got to me. It's a masterpiece."

"I'm sure the radio's going to be playing it on the constant when it comes out."

She nodded her agreement as she watched his performance come to an end.

Blaise looked at the cheering crowd and gave them a broad smile. "*Sealed with a Kiss* is dedicated to my mountain woman."

Had she heard him correctly?

If she hadn't, the camera panning to view Deola with her lips pressed into a tight line confirmed it.

Lamisi stared at the screen. Breathing didn't come easy as her chest tightened. The song had been for her. He'd created and sung it just for her.

The floor developed trampoline-like properties as she did high-knee jogs while squealing. She ignored her brother's look of incredulity as she jumped side to side and waved her hands high.

Breathing heavy and grinning so hard that her cheeks were starting to hurt, she flung her arms around herself and squeezed.

"What's gotten into you? One minute you look ready to cry, the next you're all manic. Do I need to call Mom and Dad to take you to the hospital?"

"For a case of extreme happiness? No." When his drawn brows didn't relax, she added, "I'm mountain woman. We first met on Mt. Afadjato."

Nodding, Amadu joined her with the grinning. "Now you can stop being so crabby."

"Hey, I wasn't—" Why bother to deny it? Being without Blaise had turned her into a grouch.

"Sorry," she said. It would've been a better apology without the ear-to-ear smile she still sported.

"No problem. It's good to see you happy. So, what happened between you and Blaise to get you down?"

"I was dumb."

He stumbled backwards and gasped three times in a row. "Are you admitting that women can be the cause of relationship breakdowns? I'm sure you can't tell, but I'm shocked."

The giggles wouldn't stop bubbling out of her.

Her phone pinged, indicating a text. She picked it up. Blaise.

'Did you watch my performance?'

She flicked a gaze to her brother.

"Thanks for informing about Blaise's performance."

Amadu chuckled. "Tell him he hit it hard. He's got a for sure number one on his hands."

"Just get out."

As soon as the door clicked shut, she tapped into her phone.

'*Yes.*'

Blaise: *And…*

Lamisi: *Amadu told me to tell you that you've got a #1 hit on your hands*

Blaise: *Tell him I said thanks. What did you think?*

Should she play with him or get to the point? How fragile was his ego about his music? May as well find out.

Lamisi: *I didn't cover my ears when you sang in French*

Blaise: ☺ *All thanks to you. What about the lyrics?*

The moment of truth.

Lamisi: *Even though you plagiarized yourself from the texts, they were beautiful. I thought so when they were words on my phone, but you singing them brought them new meaning. I loved the song, Blaise. You're an amazing musician*

When a response didn't come after a couple of minutes, she settled in to watch the award show while keeping a strict eye out for Blaise. She wished she could be seated next to him.

She didn't care if the world knew they were together as long as she could spend time with him. Appreciate his considerate and seemingly carefree nature. Laugh with and adore him until … Hopefully, neither would get tired of the other.

Her phone played her favourite song of Blaise's. She'd have to get a hold of his new one and swap the ringtone.

Biting down on the inside of her cheek while her heart did dangerous things in her chest, she put the TV on mute and answered. "Hello?"

"I'm glad my number one fan liked the song."

Applause and people hooting filtered through the phone, corresponding with the activity on her television.

"It's always important to keep a mountain woman happy. You never know the consequences."

Their laughter merged.

"I'd like to see you tonight, but the awards ceremony seems like it's going to last forever."

Last year, it took five hours. "You have to stay and grab your award for Artiste of the Year."

"There's no guarantee I'll win. The competition is intense."

Such a humble man. Something she hadn't expected him to be before they'd first met, and it increased her respect for him.

"Yeah, but you're the best out of all of them. That award is yours. Make sure you have your speech ready. No bumbling around on the stage so that they cut to the adverts on you."

He chuckled. "I wish you were here."

"Me, too." She twirled a strand of her hair around her finger. "We both know I would've declined the invitation if you'd asked earlier."

"True. We need to talk, Lamisi."

They sure did. "Okay."

"How about if I pick you up tomorrow at around one and we'll have lunch."

"Sounds good. I have a couple of things to take care of in the morning."

He didn't need to know that she would've skipped out on washing her clothes to see him again. She had some apologizing and explaining to do.

"I take it," she continued. "You'll be partying for the rest of the night and will sleep the morning away."

An aspect of his life her introverted personality would have to get used to.

"Huh. Everyone calls me the old man, and that's when they're being nice. I'm a homebody. It's why my house is filled with so many expensive toys. I attend parties to show my face and meet the key players. Once that's done, I'm out."

She could handle that. "Try to enjoy yourself a little, old man."

He did a combination groan and chuckle. "I probably shouldn't have shared."

Things on his end started getting loud as music blasted through the air. "Nope."

"I've got to go," he shouted into the phone. "Text me your address."

"Okay. Have fun." *But not too much.*

"Thanks. Have a good night, mountain woman."

The unromantic nickname made her ecstatic. "You, too, King of Francohip."

His laughter tickled her ear as he hung up.

Thing between them had gone from miserable to getting so good. Love was pure power.

CHAPTER THIRTY-TWO

If Blaise didn't settle down, he'd crash his car before reaching Lamisi. He wrapped his fingers around the steering wheel to stop the repetitive cracking of his knuckles. Willing himself to keep his backside still, his leg no longer propelled the vehicle faster than he intended.

The computerized voice told him to take a right. Another turn had him on a wide dirt path where the road had yet to be paved. She'd mentioned that she still lived at home with her parents and two of her siblings. Would he get to meet any of them?

He wanted to be with her. If he had to chat up every member of her family to make it happen, then he would.

The app told him he'd reached his destination. Instead of calling to tell her he'd arrived, he opened the door, climbed out of his Volvo SUV, and strode to the gate. After pressing the bell, mouth dry and hands moist, he waited.

Lamisi bounded out of the house a minute later. She looked through the open slats of the large gate and waved at him.

Grinning, he returned the gesture as she let herself out.

Not even writing and recording his own songs had ever been as thrilling as this moment of finally being with Lamisi. Such a deep longing to see someone astounded him. Maybe he'd never been in love. Until now.

"Hi." She flounced towards him wearing a light blue floral dress that reached her knees.

"Hey," was all he could get out.

"Congratulations, Mr. Best Music Video of the Year, Hiplife Artiste of the Year, Record of the Year, and Artiste of the Year. A clean sweep. I told you you'd win."

He dove into the arms she held open. Their embrace was much too short as his head swelled at the pride her voice carried.

"You certainly did. Thank you for believing in me."

"It's easy to have faith in apparent talent." As if his winning the awards was an everyday event, she changed the subject. "Instead of going out, I cooked lunch. The house is all ours."

She broke eye contact and kicked at a stone. Was she worried that he'd say no? Being alone with her was his dream.

"That's if you don't mind. My food isn't as delicious as Aunty Vida's, but people have asked for another serving on occasion."

He chuckled. "I'd thought about inviting you over to try some of my home cooking."

She let him into the compound. "Next time."

Sounded like a promise. Although she seemed relaxed and happy to see him, playing it cool got harder with each moment in her presence.

He diverted his attention to the massive home. Nothing flashy, but solid. A place where five children could have their own space to explore. The interior was simply decorated and comfortable.

"I'll be right back with some water," she offered once he was seated.

He stiffened his muscles to stop himself from following her into the kitchen. Taking in a deep breath, he reminded himself that she had allowed him to see her. A positive sign.

She returned before he could study all of the pictures filling the room. He'd spotted Lamisi right away and grinned at the child missing two front teeth in her wide smile while standing in front of a cake.

He removed the bottle of chilled water from the tray, opened it, and took a sip.

"Are you hungry? The omotuo and groundnut soup are ready."

Mashed rice formed into a ball was one of his favourites. "I'm looking forward to eating your food, but I think we should talk first."

***

Why couldn't he let them continue on the path of renewing what self-preservation had set her to destroy? She appreciated his directness and willingness to communicate, but there was no need to dive into the main topic.

"How did you produce the song you sang last night so fast?"

"Would the fact that I was motivated be an adequate answer?" he asked in a deep, smooth tone. His voice of seduction.

Heat crept up her neck and into her face. Goodness, she wished she was better at flirting. "No, it wouldn't. First tell me what motivated you and then how you got it done so quickly."

His eyes lured her into their depths. Could he see that she loved him? She didn't care if he never answered the question, as long as she could stay near him.

"You inspired me to write and record the song. I needed you to hear it so you'd understand just how serious I am about us. How much I enjoy getting to know you. You're an incredible woman, Lamisi.

Genuine, beautiful, supportive, kind, and playful. I'm a better man when I'm with you."

The sentiment must've punctured a lung because the air whooshed out of her.

She sucked in a deep breath through her nose. "Deola sent a sequence of texts saying that she was backing off. Thank you."

"I told you I'd take care of her. I promise that she'll never bother you again."

Curious, she hinged forward at the hips to get the dirt. "What did you say to her?"

His casual shrug let her know she wouldn't get the complete answer.

"We established an understanding."

Sounded rather gangster, but she wouldn't press it. Not fearing for her or her family's lives every time they opened the front door had dissipated.

Her body sang a song dedicated to him when he placed a hand on her cheek.

"Now that your life isn't at risk, are we okay? Can we get back on the dating track?"

She became weightless as everything in world clicked in place. "Yes."

Not wasting any more time, he captured her mouth in a kiss that she responded to with all the passion which flared up in her. A homecoming that made her forget why she'd ever tried to leave him. She knew for certain she wouldn't again.

Gripping the front of his shirt, she tugged him closer, opening to him. Giving and taking. Ravenous hands roamed over his shoulders. She took in his unique scent and minty taste as she absorbed his essence and gave hers freely.

She moaned, letting the perfection of the moment permeate into her.

He ended the kiss with a light brush to her lips. Pulling away, his soulful eyes gazed into hers with a concentration she adored having directed only at her.

"Lamisi, will you be my girlfriend?"

The proposal set off fireworks in her body. "Yes, Blaise."

He kissed her forehead.

"My mountain woman."

Her smile was wide with pleasure and teasing. "My old man."

"I'll never live that down, will I?"

"Nope."

Because he would always be hers.

EPILOGUE

Their section of the crowd went ballistic with cheering and hooting when Lamisi's name was announced to collect her PhD. Blaise couldn't be any prouder of her. His yells as she walked across the stage carried over the shouts of the other people who loved her.

When they'd first started dating, her family had invited him into their lives with open arms. It'd been much easier for them to accept him than it had been for Lamisi. His family, his mother especially, had loved her.

The past year had been a fast-paced whirlwind of incredible shared experiences.

They'd done their traditional Islamic wedding last month and registered at the courts to finalize it.

His career had shot off like a missile into the stratosphere.

Not only had the Francophone countries loved his French mixed music, it had caught fire everywhere. He'd approved collaboration requests from top musicians he'd only admired from afar.

Would any of it have happened if Lamisi hadn't been by his side? Yes, but it had been so much better with her in his life.

Blaise looked forward to the concert tour he had lined up. Lamisi would join him for the full three months on the road. When they got back, they'd take a couple of weeks to relax before she started her job as a lecturer at the university. She'd also spoken to a few embassies about doing translation work for them when they needed it.

At the close of the ceremony, her entourage of supporters went to meet her at the designated area.

As soon as she spotted him, her black gown billowed as she ran into his arms. He lifted her and spun her around, never wanting to let his wife go. Her clinging arms around his shoulders indicated the same.

He placed her on her feet. "I'm so proud of you, Lamisi. I love you so much."

"I love you, too, Blaise."

They gazed into each other's eyes, promises of the intimacies they'd share later raging. Their families must've decided that they'd had more than enough time to themselves and surrounded Lamisi to get in their congratulations.

Blaise had no problem sharing her. In the end, his mountain woman would go home with him.

THE END

Thank you for reading Love and Hiplife by Nana Prah. If you enjoyed this story, please leave a review on the site of purchase.

Connect with Nana: https://www.nanaprah.com/

OTHER BOOKS BY LOVE AFRICA PRESS

Twisted by Stanley Umezulike

Pharaoh's Bed by Mukami Ngari

Be My Valentine Anthology: Volume 2

Bound To Liberty by Kiru Taye

CONNECT WITH US

Facebook.com/LoveAfricaPress

Twitter.com/LoveAfricaPress

Instagram.com/LoveAfricaPress

SIGN UP TO OUR NEWSLETTER
https://www.loveafricapress.com/newsletter